Susan Slept Here

A Comedy in Two Acts

by
Steve Fisher and Alex Gottlieb

A SAMUEL FRENCH ACTING EDITION

FOUNDED 1830

New York Hollywood London Toronto

SAMUELFRENCH.COM

MUSIC USE NOTE

IMPORTANT BILLING AND CREDIT
REQUIREMENTS

CAST OF CHARACTERS

(4 males; 4 females)

MAUDE _____*Joe's secretary*
GEORGETTE _____*Joe's maid*
VIRGIL _____*Joe's friend*
JOE NORTON_____*a writer*
SERGEANT HANLON_____*of the Vice Squad*
SERGEANT MAIZEL_____*of the Vice Squad*
SUSAN LANDIS_____*a girl*
ISABELLA _____*Joe's girl*

SYNOPSIS OF SCENES

THE TIME: *The present*

THE PLACE: *Pacific Palisades, a suburb of Los Angeles*

THE SCENE: *Joe Norton's apartment*

ACT ONE

SCENE 1: *The night before Christmas*
SCENE 2: *Christmas morning*

ACT TWO

SCENE 1: *The day after Christmas*
SCENE 2: *The day before March 15th*
SCENE 3: *A day in October*

Susan Slept Here

ACT ONE

Scene 1

Scene: *Den-living room of a smart, modern home in Pacific Palisades, a suburb of Los Angeles. Since this is the home-office of a writer, its bookshelves are overloaded, and the tables are covered with magazines, scripts and more books. Even the desk, with its portable typewriter, is cluttered. The room is furnished appropriately—lots of good lamps, easy chairs, a roomy couch. The entrance is at rear Center, a door at Right leads into the kitchen, and a door at Left leads into the bedroom. Christmas presents are stacked on a table, and mistletoe hangs over the bar. The telephone, which has a long extension cord, is on the desk, as well as a framed picture of a very beautiful girl.*

At Rise: Maude *is seated at the desk, working rapidly on the portable typewriter. There is a stack of typewritten pages beside the machine.* Maude *is in her forties, a buxom woman with a good sense of humor.* Georgette, *the colored maid, is at the table, wrapping the last of the packages. She is slim, neat, and about 22. She has on her regular clothes, not a uniform.*

Maude. (*Stops typing.*) How do you spell etymology?
Georgette. E-t-y-m-o-l-o-g-y.
Maude. Thanks, Georgette. (*She types the word and pulls the paper out of the typewriter. She rises, pushing*

5

back her chair, and starts to assemble the pages of the manuscript.) Now tell me what it means.

GEORGETTE. The origin, derivation and meaning of words.

MAUDE. It certainly is nice to have an education.

GEORGETTE. What's etymology doing in a movie script?

MAUDE. This is an article for the *Saturday Review.*

GEORGETTE. I'm impressed. I thought Mr. Norton was strictly a Hollywood writer.

MAUDE. He's trying to escape.

GEORGETTE. Escape?

MAUDE. (*Crossing to the bar.*) This town is full of good writers trying to make a break over the wall. I ought to know—I've watched them for the last twenty-two years—from Mankewiecz to Mankewiecz. I wish I had a dollar for every novelist in this town who never wrote another book—or every playwright who's always going back to Broadway—and never goes. I think I'll pour myself a drink. To try and forget my wasted youth.

GEORGETTE. How does it happen you never married, Miss Maude?

MAUDE. (*Pouring drink.*) The only ones who asked me were out-of-work writers who wanted me to type their scripts. By the time the pages came hot out of the typewriter, they'd cooled off. (*Sighs.*) I'll never forgive myself for the day I took up stenography. (*Looks up at mistletoe.*) What a waste of good mistletoe.

GEORGETTE. (*Finishing package.*) Here's your Christmas present. You want it now?

MAUDE. No, thanks—I want to be surprised tomorrow when I find out it's a bottle of Aphrodisia and a check for fifty bucks. Who else is on the list this year?

GEORGETTE. (*Reading cards on packages.*) To Isabella with love. To Janet with love. To Marjorie with love. To Hedda Hopper.

MAUDE. Nothing for Louella?

GEORGETTE. Her chauffeur picked it up yesterday.

MAUDE. Oh! Why don't you run along—I'll finish those.

GEORGETTE. Thanks, but I have to wait for Ralph anyway.

MAUDE. Purely as a spectator—how is marriage?

GEORGETTE. We like it. But it does cut into our school work.

MAUDE. How are you and Ralph doing at U.C.L.A.?

GEORGETTE. He hates it because I get straight A's. But I explained to him that football players are supposed to be dumb.

(The PHONE rings. MAUDE crosses to desk to answer it, after downing her drink.)

MAUDE. *(Into phone.)* Mr. Norton's residence. *(After pause.)* No, he isn't, but I expect him shortly. Would you care to leave a message? *(Reacts.)* Who? *(Hand over mouthpiece.)* It's the police!

GEORGETTE. The police? *(Crossing to kitchen.)* I'm leaving!

MAUDE. *(Into phone.)* Oh—Sergeant Hanlon! Of course I remember you. You were technical advisor on "Guns For Sale." Yes, I thought it was a lousy picture too—*but* technically perfect. *(Listens.)* Yes, I'm sure he'll be here by then. 'Bye. *(Hangs up.)*

GEORGETTE. *(At kitchen door.)* What was that?

MAUDE. Sergeant Hanlon of the Vice Squad. He's got a present for the boss.

GEORGETTE. Why do policemen make everybody nervous?

MAUDE. Especially this one. He wants to be a writer.

GEORGETTE. Don't we all? *(She exits into the kitchen.)*

(There is a KNOCK on the door.)

VIRGIL. *(Outside apartment.)* Virgil's here! Open the door—I forgot my key.

MAUDE. It's open.

(VIRGIL *comes in. He is small, energetic, in his late twenties. At the moment his slicker and hat are dripping with water. He carries a pair of wet goggles.*)

VIRGIL. Hi! Did you ever ride a motorcycle over Coldwater Canyon in the rain? (*Looks at them.*) No, I guess not. (*Throws goggles to* MAUDE.) Here—you can hang up my goggles, if you've been a good girl.

MAUDE. I've never been anything else.

VIRGIL. Don't look at me. (*Goes to bar.*) How about a drink?

MAUDE. I never drink on the job—

VIRGIL. Oh—I forgot.

MAUDE. (*Quickly.*) —but seeing it's Christmas Eve, I'll take a short one.

(*Crosses to bar.* GEORGETTE, *wearing her raincoat and carrying galoshes, enters from the kitchen.*)

GEORGETTE. How are you, Mr. Virgil?

VIRGIL. Wet outside and planning to be the same way inside. (*Pouring drinks.*) How about you, Georgette?

GEORGETTE. (*Crossing to sit on chair by desk.*) I better not. My husband ought to be here any minute.

VIRGIL. Where does he claim he is?

GEORGETTE. (*Putting on galoshes*) I *know* where he is. He's bartending a studio party. You know how late they break up.

VIRGIL. (*Crossing to bedroom door.*) I just saw him parking the car downstairs. *His* party must've run out of liquor.

MAUDE. Sounds like Warner Brothers.

VIRGIL. (*Peers into bedroom, turns back.*) Isn't Joe here yet?

MAUDE. He didn't even phone. Maybe he got washed away in the rain.

VIRGIL. He couldn't have. He's got a date at nine.

MAUDE. With Isabella? You should pardon the expression.

VIRGIL. She's been held over.

MAUDE. She must have something.

VIRGIL. If she ever did, she hasn't now.

(*There is a car HONK outside.*)

GEORGETTE. That's Ralph. (*Crossing to Right table.*) Please tell Mr. Norton "thank you" for my extra check.

VIRGIL. *I* wrote them for everybody—including me.

GEORGETTE. I fixed a plate of sandwiches in the kitchen. The kind you like.

MAUDE. Don't forget your presents.

(GEORGETTE *picks up a huge stack of wrapped presents from a side table. She almost staggers from their weight.*)

VIRGIL. You're sure you've got everything?

GEORGETTE. I think so. (*Crossing to front door.*) Merry Christmas, everybody.

VIRGIL. (*Opening door for her.*) Merry Christmas. See you day after tomorrow.

MAUDE. Merry Christmas to you and Ralph.

(GEORGETTE *exits.* MAUDE *comes over with drinks for herself and* VIRGIL.)

VIRGIL. Well—what'll we drink to?

MAUDE. Why don't we drink to you?

VIRGIL. I like that.

MAUDE. (*Toasting.*) To Virgil—who's old enough now to go out in the world and tie his own shoelaces.

VIRGIL. I don't like *that.* You're not going to start in again, are you? (*On the defensive.*) I'm doing a good job for Joe.

MAUDE. Sure you are. But how about for yourself?

VIRGIL. I don't have time to think about it.

MAUDE. You ought to take time—one of these days.

(*They turn as they hear a key in the door. It opens and* JOE *enters. He is drenched, wears a sports jacket and no hat. He brushes back his wet hair, closes the door.*)

JOE. It's raining.

VIRGIL. That's what I like about you writers—always there with a fast epigram. (*Accusingly.*) Do you know you've got a date at nine?

JOE. (*Shedding wet jacket.*) I hope it's with my doctor. I think I caught pneumonia. (*Throws jacket to* VIRGIL.)

MAUDE. (*Holding glass apologetically.*) Virgil forced a little brandy down my throat.

VIRGIL. (*To* JOE.) What happened to you?

JOE. My car broke down. The hydramatic.

(*Kicks off wet shoes and* VIRGIL *picks them up.*)

VIRGIL. I wouldn't have a Cadillac if you gave it to me.

MAUDE. *I* would.

(VIRGIL *exits into bedroom with wet jacket and shoes.*)

JOE. (*Crossing to desk and looking at script pages.*) How's the stuff you typed?

MAUDE. I don't want to spoil your Christmas. (*She picks up her raincoat and umbrella.*)

JOE. (*Helping her on with coat.*) That bad?

MAUDE. Pretty dull.

JOE. Magazine articles are supposed to be dull.

MAUDE. Then you're a cinch for the Pulitzer Prize.

JOE. (*Crosses to the packages piled up on the table.*) Are you trying to tell me I ought to take the assignment at M-G-M?

MAUDE. No, but you can tell me something. Why would they want to make a musical out of "Lady Chatterley's Lover"?

JOE. (*Handing her package.*) Don't forget your present.

MAUDE. (*Takes it, reads tag.*) "Merry Christmas to Maude." You do write well.

JOE. Thanks. How's your mother?

MAUDE. She's still hoping somebody'll give me a man for Christmas. (*Crosses to front door.*)

JOE. How does it look?

MAUDE. (*Turning.*) Looks like there ain't no Santy Claus.

JOE. Well—stay sober tonight.

VIRGIL. (*Enters from bedroom with* JOE'S *dressing gown and slippers. To* MAUDE.) Get good and drunk tonight.

MAUDE. Don't think I haven't tried that too. Well, Merry Christmas, you-all. (*Exits.*)

VIRGIL. (*Helping* JOE *into robe.*) When's your car going to be ready?

JOE. Tomorrow.

VIRGIL. Christmas Day?

JOE. The mechanic's a friend of mine. He's doing it for only fifty bucks extra.

VIRGIL. He's a real pal.

JOE. (*Sitting down on couch to put on slippers.*) This guy has four kids. You try having four kids this time of year.

VIRGIL. I don't even smoke. Your friends really love to clip you.

JOE. I'm used to them.

VIRGIL. The only real friends a guy ever has are his shipmates.

JOE. Aren't you ever going to get out of the Navy?

VIRGIL. (*Mistily.*) My happiest days!

JOE. (*Feeling beard to see if he needs shave.*) I thought Yale was.

VIRGIL. Dear old Yale! My happiest days.

(JOE *begins to sing "Boola Boola" as he starts for bedroom.*)

(*Annoyed.*) Are you knocking a college education—just because you didn't have one?

JOE. I wouldn't dare. (*Exits.*)

(*There is a KNOCK on the door.* VIRGIL *looks over questioningly, then crosses to door and opens it. Two men, dressed in slickers and hats, stand dripping wet in the hallway. They are* HANLON *and* MAIZEL, *detectives on the Vice Squad.*)

VIRGIL. (*Showing no recognition.*) Sorry—the Christmas party must be down the street.

(*Starts to close door, but* HANLON *barges in with* MAIZEL.)

HANLON. Hanlon. I phoned up.

VIRGIL. Who?

HANLON. Hanlon, from the Vice Squad.

VIRGIL. (*Startled.*) We don't have any—

MAIZEL. They don't have any vice here, Sam.

VIRGIL. (*Sudden recognition.*) Oh—*Sergeant* Hanlon!

HANLON. In the flesh.

MAIZEL. (*Indicating* HANLON.) The author of "Guns For Sale"—October 1952 issue of Ten-Cent Detective.

VIRGIL. Just my luck—I missed that issue. (*To* HANLON.) Weren't you technical adviser on Joe's picture?

HANLON. I sure was! Ten weeks—at a hundred clams a week!

MAIZEL. (*To* VIRGIL.) Who are you?

HANLON. Virgil.

VIRGIL. (*Starting for bedroom.*) I'll tell Joe you're here.

MAIZEL. (*To* HANLON.) What does *he* do here?

HANLON. Works for Joe. He's his— (*Pauses, looks at* VIRGIL, *who has stopped and turned back.*)

VIRGIL. —assistant.

HANLON. I always meant to ask you. What does an assistant writer do? Write?

VIRGIL. Does a prize-fight manager fight?

HANLON. That's a thought.

VIRGIL. I pay his bills—run his errands—buy his Christmas presents. The main thing I do is listen to his ideas.

HANLON. Where'd he ever get a guy like you?

VIRGIL. In the Navy. I was his commanding officer.

MAIZEL. (*Studying him critically.*) You don't look like a Navy man!

VIRGIL. I went in right after I got out of Yale.

HANLON. (*Relaxing on couch.*) This job must be quite a letdown.

VIRGIL. There was an emergency in Joe's life. I couldn't desert one of my own crew.

MAIZEL. What kind of an emergency?

VIRGIL. (*Indicating picture on desk.*) Her.

MAIZEL. (*Picks up picture.*) Nice-lookin' tomato.

VIRGIL. She was his girl for six years.

HANLON. Oh—that's Maxine?

MAIZEL. (*Starting for bar.*) Is that the bar?

VIRGIL. And that's the liquor in the bottles.

HANLON. (*Indicating picture.*) Joe used to talk about her when we were writin' the picture. What happened?

VIRGIL. Did you ever go with a girl for six years?

HANLON. My wife wouldn't let me.

VIRGIL. She thought Joe was going to marry her.

HANLON. What did Joe think?

(MAIZEL *picks out a bottle at the bar.*)

VIRGIL. Joe thinks marriage is for married people.

HANLON. Where's she now?

VIRGIL. She ran off and married an actor she'd known for only two weeks. I better tell Joe you're here. He's getting dressed. (*Exits into bedroom.*)

MAIZEL. (*Pouring himself a drink.*) Do you think this is such a good idea?

HANLON. (*Crossing to bar.*) Good? Why, de Maupassant—he was the French O. Henry—he never had a better one.

MAIZEL. I ain't so sure.

HANLON. Well, I am. (*Picks up book on coffee table.*) Here's one of Joe's novels. Written by him.

MAIZEL. (*Looking at back of book.*) That him—with the open shirt?

HANLON. You ever see Hemingway with a tie on? Listen to this. (*Reads from book jacket as he sits in chair down Left.*) "At the age of sixteen Joe Norton ran off and joined the Navy. When he was discharged at the ripe old age of twenty, he had accumulated more than one hundred rejection slips, but he was determined to be a writer. He starved in Greenwich Village, washed dishes in the Automat and wrote for the WPA Theatre, before he clicked. Since then he has written several novels, two Broadway plays and many Hollywood movies. During the war he served in the Pacific. In this book, *Memory of Hell,* he draws from his experiences of those days."

VIRGIL. (*Entering from bedroom.*) Joe'll be out in a minute. (*To* MAIZEL, *who is pouring himself another, larger drink.*) How's the brandy holding up?

HANLON. Brandy! Do me a favor—hide the bottle. (*Crosses to bar and takes bottle away from* MAIZEL.) He's murder when he's loaded.

MAIZEL. (*Crosses to chair and sit moodily.*) A guy could live if they'd let him.

VIRGIL. Joe wants to know what's on your mind.

HANLON. Well—it's Christmas, and we got a present for him. Ain't we, Monty?

MAIZEL. I think this whole idea stinks.

VIRGIL. What did you get for Joe? He's got everything.

HANLON. He ain't got this. (*Rises and starts for front door.*) I'll run downstairs and get it.

VIRGIL. Why didn't you bring it up with you?

(JOE *enters from bedroom. He now wears a pair of trousers, a white shirt open at the collar, and is busy tying a tie.*)

HANLON. (*Turning back.*) Well! My favorite collaborator!

JOE. (*Crossing to* HANLON.) Sam—how are you? (*Shakes hands.*) Merry Christmas.

HANLON. Hi-ya, Joe. How's the writin' game?

JOE. A living.

HANLON. Shake hands with Monty Maizel, my partner in crime.

JOE. (*Shaking hands.*) Glad to know you.

MAIZEL. Likewise, I'm sure.

JOE. (*To* HANLON.) Tell me, Sam, how is it in Narcotics these days?

HANLON. I switched over to the Vice Squad. More interesting material.

MAIZEL. Yeah—juvenile delinquents.

HANLON. You wouldn't believe what goes on.

JOE. (*Starts quickly for bedroom.*) You must tell me about it sometime. Virgil, why don't you give these guys a drink?

HANLON. Joe, bein' it's Christmas, we got you a little—

(JOE *exits into bedroom without hearing* HANLON.) I hate to spring it on him cold.

VIRGIL. (*Lying down on couch.*) Tell me what it is. I can keep a secret.

HANLON. You think I oughta?

MAIZEL. Go on and tell him. The hell with this surprise business.

VIRGIL. Yeah—the hell with this surprise business.

HANLON. (*Crossing to sit in chair near* VIRGIL.) Well—it's like this. When I was workin' with Joe at the studio, he used to talk about an idea he had. For a play. About a juvenile delinquent.

VIRGIL. "Street Girl"?

HANLON. Yeah, that's the one. He done it yet?

VIRGIL. He's writing articles for the *Saturday Review*.

HANLON. As bad as that!

VIRGIL. He hasn't done any real writing since Maxine left.

HANLON. Well, when we were kickin' the springboard around, Joe said he'd like to come down and meet some of those sixteen-seventeen-year-old kids we pick up.

VIRGIL. What did he have in mind?

HANLON. Research—for the play. I'm a firm believer in research in my own work.

VIRGIL. Are you now?

HANLON. Yesterday we got a pickup order from downtown on a kid. Old man's dead and her mother ran off with some guy. This j.d. is—

VIRGIL. J.d.?

HANLON. Juvenile delinquent. Don't they teach you anything at Yale? This j.d.'s only seventeen, so she'll spend the next four years on the prison farm.

VIRGIL. What's all this got to do with us?

HANLON. Well, it's Christmas Eve, and me and Monty's got sentiments just like people.

MAIZEL. Yeah.

HANLON. We figured it wasn't right for her to spend Christmas in the jug.

MAIZEL. We're sick and tired of everybody sayin' cops on the Vice Squad are such rats.

HANLON. When you meet this kid, you'll see she's great material for Joe's play.

VIRGIL. You know, the Theatre Guild could use a man like you.

MAIZEL. We got our own union.

HANLON. It's holy hell downtown tonight. Might take us three hours to get her booked, and it's late already. So I got to thinkin', why couldn't we say we didn't find her until the day after Christmas?

MAIZEL. Sort of a little white lie.

HANLON. It's a real O. Henry twist. I bring this kid up here—you let her stay with your mother tonight—

VIRGIL. (*Sitting up with a start.*) My mother lives in Ohio.

HANLON. Well, you can put the kid in a room somewhere. If I know Joe, he'll see she gets a good Christmas dinner.

VIRGIL. What happens after that?

MAIZEL. The day after Christmas she goes to the farm.

HANLON. (*Crossing to front door.*) I'll go down and get her—we got her handcuffed to the steering wheel.

MAIZEL. We didn't want her to be uncomfortable.

(HANLON *exits.*)

VIRGIL. And to think today started out like any other day. (*Crossing to bar.*) Do you mind if I have a drink?

MAIZEL. No—go right ahead.

JOE. (JOE *enters from the bedroom, fully dressed in a dark suit. He carries a topcoat that he tosses on chair down Left. Looking around.*) Where did Sam go?

MAIZEL. He's got a Christmas present for you in the car.

VIRGIL. Locked to the steering wheel.

JOE. I'll call Isabella and tell her I'll be late. (*Goes to phone, dials.*) A Christmas present? Sam shouldn't have done it.

VIRGIL. We didn't get anything for him.

JOE. (*Hanging up.*) Line's busy. (*To* MAIZEL.) You don't mind if I rush off? I've got a date with a girl.

MAIZEL. You sure have.

JOE. (*Dialing phone again.*) I'm calling her now.

VIRGIL. He doesn't mean Isabella.

JOE. (*Hanging up, annoyed.*) Still busy. How can women talk so long on the phone?

MAIZEL. You're lucky you got a lot of numbers. All *I* got is my wife and Headquarters.

VIRGIL. Not us. We run a welfare agency. The kid here's a humanitarian. Specializes in stray cats and birds with broken wings. Would you like a list of the people he loaned money to who won't even talk to him now?

JOE. (*Who has been dialing again.*) Got it. (*Into phone.*) Hello, Isabella—who you been talking to so long? (*Pause.*) Oh—you were trying to dial me?

(*The front door bursts open and* HANLON *pushes in a small blonde, wearing a cheap yellow rain slicker and matching hat. She is quite pretty, but at the moment,* SUSAN LANDIS, *age 17, is quite bedraggled.* HANLON, *putting a pair of handcuffs in his pocket, closes the door, stands with his back against it.* SUSAN *looks around at the men, frightened and suspicious.*)

HANLON. This is Susie.

MAIZEL. (*Rising.*) Rhymes with floozie.

SUSAN. Where is she?

HANLON. Now take it easy.

SUSAN. (*Half-hysterical.*) Where is she?

HANLON. (*To* OTHERS.) I told her my mother lived here. Otherwise she wouldn't get out of the car.

JOE. (*Into phone.*) I'll have to call you back, Isabella. I mean—I'll be over in a little while. (*Flustered.*) Thanks for calling—that is—goodbye. (*Hangs up.*)

HANLON. Joe—meet Susan Landis. Susan Landis— meet Joe.

(SUSAN *rushes for the front door.* HANLON *pushes her back.*)

SUSAN. Let me out of here!

HANLON. Nobody's going to hurt you.

SUSAN. Let me out!

HANLON. I said take it easy.

(SUSAN *runs toward the bedroom, but* MAIZEL *blocks her way, catches her by the arm.*)

JOE. Sam, what is this?

HANLON. You said you wanted to talk to a juvenile delinquent.

MAIZEL. And she's as delinquent as they come.

SUSAN. I want to get out of here!

JOE. Sam, what the hell is this?

VIRGIL. (*Relaxing on couch.*) He's giving her to you for Christmas.

SUSAN. (*Turning on him.*) Nobody's giving me to anybody!

MAIZEL. He was gonna hang her in a stocking and put an apple in her mouth.

VIRGIL. She's the character in your play.

JOE. What play?

VIRGIL. "Street Girl."

JOE. There isn't any such play.

HANLON. There will be. If you use her.

JOE. What could I possibly use *her* for?

HANLON. Research. Put her up somewhere tonight—talk to her tomorrow—by midnight you'll have a play.

JOE. And I've always been doing it the hard way.

SUSAN. (*Facing* JOE.) Do I get out of here or don't I?

JOE. You sure do. (*Moves her toward front door.*) You and me both. Come on—where do you live?

HANLON. (*Blocking their way.*) She don't. Unless you call a reformatory living.

JOE. What did she do?

HANLON. She hit a sailor over the head with a beer bottle.

MAIZEL. She was tryin' to launch him.

JOE. Where was the Shore Patrol?

HANLON. Who do you think she hit?

SUSAN. He had it coming to him.

JOE. Oh, be a good guy, Sam. Take her home to her mother.

HANLON. Who knows where her mother is? She took a powder.

MAIZEL. Ran off with some guy.

SUSAN. I can take care of myself.

VIRGIL. Yeah. Give her a case of Budweiser and she could sink the whole Navy.

JOE. What's a little bottle of beer among friends, Sam? Give the kid a break.

HANLON. I got my orders, Joe. She's a juvenile delinquent—no folks, no relatives. The State's gonna lock her up until she's twenty-one.

MAIZEL. It's only four years.

VIRGIL. Like a college education.

HANLON. I'm trying to do the decent thing. Christmas Eve in jail is awful.

JOE. You don't write a play in one day.

VIRGIL. (*Waving them off.*) Take her away, boys—no deal.

SUSAN. (*To* JOE.) Please—make them let me go.

JOE. How can I—they're on the Vice Squad.

SUSAN. I didn't do anything so terrible.

MAIZEL. What do you call fourteen stitches?

JOE. Well—you're under age, aren't you?

VIRGIL. Is that a crime?

HANLON. (*Trying to sell* SUSAN.) I got kids and a tree to decorate yet, and look at the time.

MAIZEL. (*To* SUSAN.) You're spoilin' our Christmas.

SUSAN. I don't care—I'm not staying here.

HANLON. We're just tryin' to do you a favor.

SUSAN. I don't want any favors from men.

VIRGIL. (*To* JOE.) I suppose I could get her a room at the Studio Club. Lots of the girls must've gone home for Christmas.

MAIZEL. She'd run away two minutes after you left her there.

VIRGIL. Of course she could stay here.

JOE. Here? Who's going to watch her? (*Looking at watch.*) I'm late as hell for Isabella already. (*Gets coat; crosses to front door.*)

VIRGIL. (*Crosses to Christmas tree.*) I've got to deliver the presents.

JOE. Take Junior with you. When you come back you can lock her in the bedroom.

SUSAN. (*Blocking his way.*) Oh no, you don't!

VIRGIL. I can't take her with me. There isn't room.

JOE. Put her in the sidecar.

VIRGIL. I'm picking up Lillian.

HANLON. (*To* JOE.) My story mind tells me you got no choice. You're going to let her stay. Right?

JOE. (*Reluctantly.*) Okay, she stays. (*To* SUSAN.) Sit down, kid. Relax.

(SUSAN *sits warily on the edge of the couch.*)

HANLON. (*To* SUSAN.) The day after Christmas, we gotta deliver you downtown. Run away and we'll find you again, you understand.

MAIZEL. You're police property now. Don't you forget that.

VIRGIL. (*As detectives move toward door.*) And don't you boys forget to come back after her.

HANLON. Day after tomorrow. (*Expansively.*) This works out great for everybody. The kid eats a fancy dinner—we get a play out of her—(*Hopefully.*)—don't we, Joe?

JOE. (*Flatly.*) Merry Christmas.

MAIZEL. (*Pausing at door.*) Remember, she's only seventeen. Lay a hand on her and that's all, brother. (*Exits.*)

HANLON. I see it as a one-set show. Not more than seven or eight characters. Otherwise it costs too much to play it on the road.

VIRGIL. How were the notices in Chicago?

(HANLON *gives him a look and exits.* SUSAN *stares at* JOE *and* VIRGIL, *who study her in turn.*)

I can't remember the last time anybody gave me a girl for Christmas. (*Starts to put on slicker and hat.*)

JOE. Where are you going?

VIRGIL. You'll have to be the baby sitter.

JOE. Oh, no!

VIRGIL. I'm playing Santa Claus for you.

SUSAN. (*Jumping up.*) I'm not staying alone in a house with a man! Two men yes, but not one!

JOE. You'll have to explain that line of reasoning to me sometime. (*To* VIRGIL.) What about Isabella?

VIRGIL. That's your problem. Lillian's waiting for me. (*Begins to pile presents in his arms.*)

SUSAN. I know what's going to happen if I stay here!

JOE. (*To* VIRGIL.) I'm already an hour late.

SUSAN. If one of you goes out of this house, so do I!

JOE. (*To* VIRGIL, *after giving* SUSAN *a look of annoyance.*) I suppose we should do something about her.

VIRGIL. (*His arms piled high.*) It's simple. You hold her while I go out the door.

JOE. (*Finally.*) Aye, aye, sir. (*Salutes.*)

SUSAN. Oh no, you don't!

(SUSAN *makes a break for the front door, but* JOE *grabs her.* VIRGIL *pulls the door open and hurries out.*)

SUSAN. (*Struggling to free herself.*) Let go of me!

JOE. Will you stay put if I do?

SUSAN. No!

(*She bites* JOE *on the hand and he pushes her aside.*)

JOE. (*Eyeing hand.*) You bit me! (*He snaps lock on the door.*)

SUSAN. Go ahead—lock the door! (*Runs to window.*) I'll jump out the window!

JOE. (*Crossing to table.*) Do you mind waiting until I phone Isabella? (*Starts to dial.*)

SUSAN. (*Struggling to open window.*) When they pick up my bruised and bleeding body, I'll tell them what you were trying to do!

JOE. Oh, stop dramatizing yourself. Grow up.

SUSAN. (*Turning from window.*) I am grown up. I'm grown up enough to know why they brought me here.

(JOE *hangs up.*)

All that stuff about using me for research—so you can write a play!

JOE. Do you think a man my age has to go to all this trouble for—

SUSAN. I don't know any men your age. And I don't want to.

JOE. That makes two of us. Now relax until Virgil gets back.

(SUSAN *sits on the couch and studies him intently as he crosses to the bar.*)

Stop looking at me like I'm Jack the Ripper. Take off your hat and coat.

SUSAN. Remember what that cop said—I'm seventeen and don't you lay a hand on me!

(JOE *gives her a look and pours himself a drink.* SUSAN, *never taking her eyes off him, takes off her slicker and hat without getting up.*)

JOE. Cigarettes in front of you there.

SUSAN. I've never smoked.

JOE. (*Crossing to her with drink.*) Would you like a drink?

SUSAN. (*With an accusing finger.*) You want to get me drunk!

JOE. Yes—I want to get you drunk.

(*She looks at him and jumps up to put on her hat and slicker.* JOE *helps her on with the slicker, buttons it up and jams the hat down on her head over her ears.*)

There! You feel safer now? (*As she doesn't answer.*) You get so dramatic about everything. You ought to be an actress.

SUSAN. I am an actress. Did you ever see "Coquette"?

JOE. With Helen Hayes?

SUSAN. With Susan Landis.

JOE. No—I seldom get out to Glendale High.

SUSAN. (*Surprised.*) It was Eagle Rock High. How did you know?

JOE. I'm psychic. Were you good in the play?

SUSAN. My mother cried for three acts.

JOE. That's par for the course. (*Sitting on arm of couch.*) You could be an actress all right—with your heroic complex.

SUSAN. (*Facing him.*) What does that mean?

JOE. You make yourself think you're important.

SUSAN. What's wrong with that?

JOE. Nothing at all.

SUSAN. (*Dramatically.*) You think I'm unimportant because I'm poor, don't you? Because I'm being hounded by the police! Because my mother and I practically lived in the gutter!

JOE. Sit down, Tallulah.

(SUSAN *hesitates, then sits down.*)

(*Rising to study her.*) I'd forgotten what seventeen-year-old girls were like. I've been going out with middle-aged actresses—twenty and twenty-one.

SUSAN. You talk like a writer. Are you really a writer?

JOE. (*Picks up novel, hands it to her.*) You'll think so if you don't read past the jacket.

SUSAN. Hey, I know this! My mother got it at the lending library.

JOE. (*Pleased.*) Did you like it?

SUSAN. I liked the part about the sailor and the nurse—when he was in the hospital. That was hot stuff.

JOE. (*Flatly.*) Thanks.

SUSAN. If you wrote about me, would I be in a book like your nurse—what was her name?

JOE. Margie. No—you'd be more like Nellie Forbush.

SUSAN. Who's she?

JOE. Another nurse.

SUSAN. I'm hungry.

JOE. Didn't you have dinner?

SUSAN. Oh, sure. The cops bought me four hot dogs. But usually around this hour, some creep in a dance hall is buying me a cup of coffee and a hamburger—

JOE. —and trying to get you out in his car for a little necking?

SUSAN. (*Accusingly.*) What's wrong with that?

JOE. (*Crosses toward kitchen.*) I'll get you a sandwich.

SUSAN. Where's the part where the nurse and the sailor decide they're in love? With each other.

JOE. Page 260. (*Exits into kitchen.*)

(SUSAN *looks around, surveys the apartment appreciatively. She picks up* JOE'S *book, starts to read at page 260, takes off her hat and slicker as she reads.*)

SUSAN. (*Calling off.*) Are you supposed to be the hero in this book?

JOE. (*From kitchen.*) My hero wasn't a hero. He was scared to death under fire and he never won a medal. (*Enters with sandwich, glass of milk, small bowl of fruit, all on a tray.*)

SUSAN. He did all right with the girls.

JOE. In that case, the book is purely autobiographical. (*Puts tray in front of* SUSAN.)

SUSAN. I was in another play.

JOE. "Victoria Regina?"

SUSAN. No. It was about a rich fellow who had ulterior motives on me.

JOE. Now why can't I think of plots like that?

SUSAN. (*Starting to eat.*) Do you think a good plot helps a story?

JOE. Well—it sort of rounds it out.

SUSAN. (*Munching on sandwich.*) Hey, this is a neat sandwich. You always keep liverwurst in the house?

JOE. I wouldn't be without it. Milk all right or would you rather have coffee?

SUSAN. Have you got any chocolate milk?

JOE. I wouldn't know. I only live here.

Susan. You married?

Joe. No.

Susan. Why not?

Joe. I've been too busy writing love stories. (*Drops into chair Right.*)

Susan. What were you going to do tonight if I hadn't come along to louse up your Christmas Eve?

Joe. See a friend of mine.

Susan. A girl?

Joe. If memory serves me.

Susan. You can still see her. Go ahead—I won't run away. I'll stay right here and eat your liverwurst and read your book till the guy with the motorcycle comes back.

Joe. Maybe I'll just sit here and watch you for a while. (*The PHONE rings. Joe crosses to answer it. Susan concentrates on her sandwich.*)

(*Into phone.*) Hello. Yes, Virgil, what's the matter? (*Listens, then exasperated.*) How could all three tires go flat at the same time? (*Listens.*) You dirty little double-crosser! And a Merry Christmas to you. (*Hangs up.*) Virgil won't be back tonight. Put your coat on.

Susan. (*Rising.*) Where are we going?

Joe. *You're* going to a motel. (*Helping her with coat.*) Will you stay put until I pick you up tomorrow?

Susan. I've never been in a motel.

Joe. The experience will do you good. (*Crosses to phone and dials.*) Hello. This is Joe Norton, in Pacific Palisades. How soon can I get a cab? (*Pause.*) Three hours? No—forget it. (*Hangs up, looks at Susan.*) No taxis—on account of the rain and Christmas Eve. (*Picks up small black book by phone, looks for a number in it.*)

Susan. Who you calling now?

Joe. *Whom.* I'll see if I've got a friend who owns a car and is still sober. (*Dials number, waits as it doesn't answer.*)

Susan. Mr. Norton—

Joe. Yes?

SUSAN. (*Indicating couch.*) I could sleep right here. In my clothes.

JOE. He's not home. (*Hangs up phone.*) That's a lousy idea. Do you mind walking in the rain?

SUSAN. (*Sitting down.*) I'll be comfortable here—really I will.

JOE. *Up!*

SUSAN. (*Rising.*) Aren't you going to let me stay and write a play about me?

JOE. No play—but it looks like I'm stuck. You can stay for the night. (*As she starts to sit again.*) In the bedroom.

SUSAN. Where will you sleep?

JOE. You just told me how comfortable the couch is. Where's your baggage?

SUSAN. All my things are in a locker at the P.E. Station. The cops wouldn't let me get them. I've been living with girl friends.

JOE. Well, Virgil can pick up your things tomorrow. (*Indicating.*) You'll find a new toothbrush and anything else you need in the bathroom. Good night.

SUSAN. (SUSAN *starts toward the bedroom, then hesitates and turns.*) I hate to take your bed.

JOE. That's all right—I don't sleep good anywhere.

SUSAN. No, it isn't all right. *I'll* sleep out here.

JOE. Get in there. (SUSAN *shrugs and exits into bedroom.* JOE *stands looking after her for a moment, then the PHONE rings. Crossing to phone.*) Yes, Virgil—what is it now? (*Pause, then weakly.*) Oh, hello, Isabella. Didn't Virgil tell you— (*Pause.*) You'll never believe why I'm not coming over. I have to stay here and take care of a girl.

(*The receiver is apparently slammed up on him. He rubs his ear and hangs up, starts for bar but the PHONE rings again. He turns back and answers it.*) She's a juvenile delinquent. The police brought her up here! (*Listens.*) Isabella, you have one of the dirtiest little minds I ever—

(*Again the receiver is banged down, this time harder than before. He hangs up, starts for bar. He reaches for his drink just as the PHONE rings again. He drinks while it rings, and then goes over and answers it.*)

She's twelve years old and a chronic nymphomaniac! Any more questions? (*Pause as he listens.*) Virgil did all the shopping—how do I know what possessed him to buy you a Mexican rebosa? (*Listens.*) Yes, I *know* we're way past the rebosa stage. Sure—leave it outside your door. I'll have Virgil pick it up in the morning. (*Hangs up.*)

    (SUSAN *appears in bedroom doorway.*)

(*Turns and glares at her.*) I thought you'd gone to bed.

SUSAN. I'm scared to go to bed.

JOE. What are you scared of?

SUSAN. I'm afraid I'll fall asleep.

(JOE *looks at her for a long moment, then starts toward* SUSAN *and walks right past her into the bedroom. She takes a hesitant step after him, not sure if he wants her to follow. Then she suddenly starts for the front door.* JOE *appears in the doorway, carrying a flannel robe.*)

JOE. Where do you think you're going?

SUSAN. Now I *am* scared!

JOE. What the hell's the matter with you! You're just cold. (*Tosses robe to her.*) Here—put this on.

SUSAN. (*Weakly.*) Put it on?

JOE. I never like to play cards with a girl unless she's nice and warm. (*Crosses to get cards and a pad from the desk.*)

SUSAN. Cards? I never read any stories where—

JOE. (*Interrupting.*) Gin rummy—until I feel sleepy.

SUSAN. I don't play gin rummy.

JOE. You play canasta?

SUSAN. No.

JOE. Tiddle-winks? (SUSAN *shakes her head.*) Okay,

I'll teach you how to play gin. (*Clears space on coffee table for cards, motions for* SUSAN *to sit down on ottoman.*)

SUSAN. Yes, sir.

JOE. Okay—what'll we play for?

SUSAN. (*After thinking about it.*) Why don't we play for who gets the bedroom and who sleeps out here?

JOE. Okay. (*Starts to deal.*)

SUSAN. What if it's a tie?

JOE. (*Caught dealing in mid-air, gives her a look.*) Now the object of the game is you deal ten cards to each player— (*Continues to deal.*)

CURTAIN

ACT ONE

SCENE 2

SCENE: *It is the next morning.*

A figure is lying curled up on the couch, completely covered by a blanket. The PHONE rings, and finally JOE *sits up on his elbows. The PHONE rings insistently again, and he starts to roll off the couch but quickly lies down again and pretends to be sleeping as* SUSAN *hurries out of the kitchen and answers the phone. She wears a pair of* JOE'S *pajamas, with the sleeves and legs rolled up. She speaks very low in order not to disturb* JOE.

SUSAN. (*Into phone.*) Hello. Mr. Norton—(*Looks over at him.*)—is still sleeping. (*Pause.*) No, it isn't Georgette. (*Pause.*) No, it isn't Maude. Who is this? (*She listens.*) Isabella?

(JOE *reacts.*)

I'm Susan Landis. (*Listens.*) I've been here all night.

(JOE *holds his hand to his head.*)

I'd rather not disturb him right now—we had a pretty rough session. *(Pause, then indignantly.)* We played gin rummy. I beat him fifteen straight games. *(Listens.)* Yes, that's all. I'll be happy to tell him you called.

(*She hangs up, exits into kitchen.* JOE *rises quickly, hurries into bedroom just as* SUSAN *enters from kitchen with tablecloth and utensils.*)

(Calls toward bedroom.) Mr. Norton?

JOE. *(From bedroom.)* Is that you, Susan?

SUSAN. (SUSAN *picks up the blanket, starts to fold it.*) Who did you expect—Georgette, or Maude, or Isabella?

JOE. *(From bedroom.)* Good morning!

SUSAN. Good morning! Would you like some coffee?

JOE. *(From bedroom.)* I sure would. How are you?

SUSAN. I'm fine. You snore.

JOE. (JOE *appears in bedroom doorway, his shirt is off, a towel around his shoulders.*) How would you know?

SUSAN. I came in during the night to see if you were covered up.

JOE. Was I?

SUSAN. Yes. Go comb your hair. And put a shirt on.

JOE. Yes, Mother. *(Starts for bedroom, turns at doorway.)* What was that about Georgette and Maude and Isabella?

SUSAN. The last one called and she thought I was the other two.

JOE. How did you explain your being here to Isabella?

SUSAN. I didn't. She a friend of yours?

JOE. You might say that. Why?

SUSAN. Your friend has a dirty mind. She ought to have her mouth washed out with soap.

JOE. What did she say?

SUSAN. *(Hands him the pillow and blanket.)* Put your shoes on. You'll catch cold in your bare feet.

JOE. Thank you, Virgil.

(*He exits into bedroom.* SUSAN *starts to lay out the cloth and silverware on the coffee table.*)

SUSAN. Can you hear me?

JOE. (*From bedroom.*) You're coming in nice and clear.

SUSAN. Still mad at me?

JOE. (*From bedroom.*) Mad at you? What about?

SUSAN. The gin rummy game.

JOE. (*From bedroom.*) Oh—that. Beginner's luck. You're my pigeon from now on.

(*The PHONE rings.*)

SUSAN. Shall I answer it?

JOE. (*From bedroom.*) You know how?

SUSAN. (*Crossing to phone.*) Hello—Mr. Norton's residence—yes, I'm still here. (*After pause.*) I haven't got a home. Why don't you take a flying—

JOE. (*From bedroom.*) Who's on the phone?

SUSAN. (*Into receiver.*) Your friend with the dirty mind.

JOE. (*From bedroom.*) Tell her I'll call her back as soon as I get dressed.

SUSAN. (*Into phone.*) He'll call you back as soon as he gets dressed. (*Hangs up, crosses toward kitchen.*)

JOE. (*From bedroom.*) Where would you like to go for breakfast?

(SUSAN *smiles, hurries into kitchen just as* JOE *appears in bedroom doorway, wearing slacks and sports shirt, and carrying a jacket.*)

I said where would you like to— (*Stops as he realizes he's alone, crosses quickly and opens front door.*) Susan! Susan!

SUSAN. (SUSAN *appears in kitchen doorway. She carries a tray with two cups of coffee, cream and sugar.*) Quiet—the neighbors!

JOE. (*Turning and closing door.*) I thought you'd run away.

SUSAN. How do you like your coffee?

JOE. (*Crosses to table and sits.*) Black—and it better be good.

SUSAN. It is.

JOE. (*Takes sip of coffee, reacts with surprise.*) Hey!

SUSAN. Domestic Science class. Straight A's for three years. (*Sits chair Right.*)

JOE. Miss Landis, you're the best actress-cook to come out of Eagle Rock this semester.

SUSAN. Oh, anybody can cook. That's what my mother always said.

JOE. Did you make coffee for your mother?

SUSAN. Whenever she had a hangover.

JOE. Was that often?

SUSAN. Don't get me wrong—she really didn't drink a lot. (*Crosses to couch and sits on top of it.*) You have to understand about Mom. She was more like my girl friend than my mother. She was only seventeen when I was born. Mom always seems so young to me, but I guess she isn't really. She's thirty-four.

JOE. (*Gulping on coffee.*) That's old?

SUSAN. Isn't it?

JOE. I'm thirty-four.

SUSAN. (*Surprised.*) You're thirty-four?

JOE. (*Confidentially.*) Don't kick it around, will you? I tell everybody I'm twenty-nine. (*Nicely.*) Where's your mother now, Susan?

SUSAN. Like those creeps told you, she ran off with a guy.

JOE. Is she pretty?

SUSAN. She's beautiful. She's small and blonde, like me. She's a Texas girl, from El Paso. I was born there too.

JOE. Tell me some more about her.

SUSAN. Well, Mom never worried about being poor. All she ever worried about was love.

JOE. All women worry about love.

SUSAN. Not like Mom. My Mom and Dad loved each other an awful lot. But after I was born, everything seemed to change.

JOE. How do you know how everything was before you were born?

SUSAN. Mom told me. You see, my Dad came out of an orphan home. He wanted to be the best father in the world. So he showered all his love and affection on me. Poor Mom—she was left out in the cold. (*Crosses to table and picks up* JOE'S *empty cup.*) More coffee?

JOE. Thanks.

(SUSAN *exits into kitchen.*)

Are they divorced now?

SUSAN. (*From kitchen.*) They were divorced when I was seven. I sure loused things up for my mother.

JOE. Where's your father now?

SUSAN. He's dead. (*Appearing in doorway.*) He died alone—in Chicago. He hated Chicago—especially in the winter. He missed California, but he didn't want to live here and not be allowed to see me except weekends. Whoever decides those divorce agreements that cut up a kid into weekdays and weekends ought to have a talk with the kid first.

JOE. It must have been pretty tough on you, loving both parents.

SUSAN. It was toughter for my mother. (*Entering with coffee.*) After my father died, she worked in a cheap cafe to support us. (*Puts coffee before* JOE.) Where you meet only the kind of men who think every waitress is a pickup. (*Crossing to couch and sitting on top of it again.*) Poor Mom—she fell for so many phonies.

JOE. Who's the phoney she ran off with?

SUSAN. He's no phoney—he's the real thing!

JOE. (*Dryly.*) He must be—running off with your mother—leaving you like this.

SUSAN. I made them do it.

JOE. You did what?

SUSAN. This fellow—his name's Joe too—he had to go to Peru on a construction job, but he didn't have enough money to take both of us—and it was Mom's last chance. I told her to grab it.

JOE. What did she expect would happen to you?

SUSAN. Do you know what Mom's been doing?

JOE. I don't believe I do.

SUSAN. Working in a taxi-dance hall on Main Street. Every night she'd come home and play records about love—on our portable phonograph—and cry. Then she met this Joe. I told her I'd get a job. I'll be all right.

JOE. Sure. You'll be the only girl on the prison farm who gets mail from Peru. Save the stamps for me, will you?

SUSAN. You don't realize what I owe my mother. The night I was born, she almost died.

JOE. What makes you think it was your fault if she had? And it wasn't your fault your father stopped loving your mother. Don't you see what your mother's done to you?

SUSAN. What are you talking about?

JOE. She reversed your relationships. She became the child and made you the mother.

SUSAN. (*Crossing to table.*) You need some more coffee.

JOE. She wanted you to think of her as your girl friend. Because you were a substitute—for the love and protection she wanted.

SUSAN. Well, she's got it now.

JOE. And what have you got?

SUSAN. I'm younger and stronger than she is.

JOE. You're younger and dumber!

SUSAN. How did I know the cops were going to pick me up?

(*She starts to pick up the dishes as* JOE *gets up and paces, then turns to eye her.*)

JOE. Do you know how to make a three-minute egg?

SUSAN. I have a wonderful recipe.

JOE. Go out in the kitchen and make me one. (*Crossing to phone decisively.*) I'm going to call my lawyer.

SUSAN. If it's about me, you're wasting your time. They explained it all to me.

JOE. My three-minute egg please.

(SUSAN *shrugs and exits into kitchen as* JOE *dials.*) (*Into phone.*) Hello, Virgil. How's the pride and joy of Harley-Davidson this morning? (*Listens briefly.*) I'm glad *you* slept well. Have you got my lawyer's unlisted number in your little black book? Well, call him and tell him all about Susan. I want him to pull every string to keep her out of that finishing school for wayward girls. On the way over here, pick up that Mexican bit I gave Isabella. She doesn't seem to go for it. And stop at Janet's—she's about the same size as the kid—and borrow some clothes for her. (*Listens.*) She didn't go to a motel. She slept in my bed. (*Listens, then indignantly.*) On the couch! (*Hangs up.*)

SUSAN. (*From kitchen.*) Minute and a quarter to go.

JOE. Virgil's calling my lawyer.

SUSAN. (*Entering from kitchen.*) How do you want your toast?

JOE. Toasted.

SUSAN. Marmalade or jelly? You have both kinds.

JOE. Aren't you even a little worried about what might happen to you? Tomorrow you could be on a prison farm. For years!

SUSAN. Don't you understand, Mr. Norton? I can't afford to live in the future.

JOE. Did that line come out of you?

SUSAN. I read it in a book once.

JOE. It must have been a lousy book.

SUSAN. You should know. You wrote it. The marine said that when they went ashore at Iwo Jima.

JOE. He was stupid.

SUSAN. What are you so upset about? This is the nicest Christmas morning I've ever known. I wish I had a present for you.

JOE. Tie a ribbon around the eggs and write "From me to you" on them.

SUSAN. Oh, your eggs!

(*She rushes back into the kitchen.* JOE *stands looking after her, then walks to the desk, picks up the article he wrote, reads a paragraph, makes a pained face, tears the article in two and drops the pages into the wastebasket.*)

(*From kitchen.*) I'm afraid they're three-and-a-half minutes.

(JOE *sits down gloomily at the table.* SUSAN *enters with a tray bearing an egg cup, the eggs, salt and pepper shakers, and two pieces of buttered toast.*)

(*Aware of his mood.*) I'm sorry I spoiled the eggs.

JOE. It's all right. What difference can half a minute make?

(SUSAN *crosses to desk and picks up Maxine's picture.* JOE *starts to unshell an egg.*)

SUSAN. Who's this—Isabella?

JOE. Hardly.

SUSAN. What's *her* name?

JOE. Maxine, and put that down.

SUSAN. Why do you keep *her* picture around if you're going with Isabella? Can't you make up your mind?

JOE. (*Irritated, takes bite of egg.*) You ruined the eggs! The extra half-minute ruins an egg!

SUSAN. I'm sorry.

JOE. Get me a drink, will you?

SUSAN. (*Crosses to bar.*) What do you have with your eggs—Scotch or bourbon?

JOE. All right—I'll get it myself. (*Rises.*) Is it a crime to have a drink on Christmas? (*Crosses to bar.*)

SUSAN. You know what? You're carrying a torch.

JOE. (*Pouring a drink.*) I always thought Dorothy Dix was an older woman.

SUSAN. You can drink all you want, but the torch won't go out. My mother told me.

JOE. Your mother talks too much. (*Aware she's hurt.*) I'm sorry I flew off the handle. The eggs are fine. Aren't you going to have any breakfast?

SUSAN. I ate before you got up. (*Sitting cross-legged on couch.*) Have you had a lot of girls?

JOE. (*Crossing back to table with drink, sits on couch.*) Ask Virgil. He keeps my diary.

SUSAN. Were you in love with them?

JOE. When you grow up, you'll discover you don't fall in love just because you want to or need to.

SUSAN. (*With accusing finger.*) Hey—you sound just like my mother!

JOE. I'd rather be dead.

SUSAN. I guess everybody needs love. Just like she did.

JOE. What do you know about who needs love?

SUSAN. You sound exactly like my mother.

JOE. That did it! (*Crosses and returns to bar with drink.*) You just put me on the wagon.

SUSAN. (*Rising and going over to* JOE.) Mr. Norton— would you like me to kiss you?

JOE. (*Backing away.*) Kiss me? Why would I want you to do that?

SUSAN. Because it's Christmas.

JOE. No. Absolutely no.

SUSAN. Well then—would *you* like to kiss *me?*

JOE. Why?

SUSAN. Because it's Christmas. (*She parks herself under the mistletoe, gets on her tiptoes and looks at him appealingly.*)

JOE. (*With a smile.*) I'd be a cad if I didn't.

(*He takes her in his arms and kisses her. The apartment door opens and* VIRGIL *enters, carrying a suit-box. He walks right across toward the bedroom.*)

VIRGIL. Hi!

JOE. (*Breaking from kiss.*) Hi!

(*He goes back into kiss.* VIRGIL *continues on, then realizes what he saw, stops, turns around.*)

VIRGIL. Elvis Presley!

(JOE *and* SUSAN *break from kiss, but* SUSAN *remains in a trance, looking awed at* JOE.)

She happens to be under age!

JOE. That was just a brotherly, Christmas kiss.

VIRGIL. Oh, brother! (*Snaps fingers under* SUSAN'S *nose.*) Some clothes for you. The pajama party's over.

(SUSAN, *still in a daze, takes the box and exits Zombie-like into bedroom.*)

(*Crossing to get a cigarette from coffee table.*) No wonder you wanted me to call your lawyer.

JOE. What did he say?

VIRGIL. He said to take a cold shower.

JOE. That's great advice.

VIRGIL. (*Pointing with cigarette.*) He thinks you're crazy. That makes two of us.

JOE. What kind of a lawyer is he! I'll get some action.

VIRGIL. Look—Greg said the law on stray juveniles is airtight. Nobody can keep her from going to the prison farm.

JOE. (*Crossing to* VIRGIL.) Farm! Do you realize those creeps are going to take her away tomorrow?

VIRGIL. The way things looked when I walked in, you'll be lucky if they don't take *you* away. (*Walks around looking for a match.*)

JOE. (*Following him.*) Do you know what happens to a girl like that when she's shut up for four years with every little female tramp in the state?

VIRGIL. (*Turning on him.*) But there's nothing you can do, Joe. Unless we adopt her. What do you want to do—adopt her? That's the only idea Greg had.

JOE. Lawyers!

VIRGIL. (*Looking in* JOE'S *empty cup on table.*) I feel like a cup of coffee. How do you feel?

JOE. Like hell.

VIRGIL. (*Crossing to kitchen.*) What really happened here last night?

JOE. Nothing. (*Spelling it out.*) N-o-t-h-i-n-g.

VIRGIL. (*Disbelieving.*) Sure. (*Spelling it out.*) S-u-r-e.

(*He exits into kitchen. There's a KNOCK on the door.
    JOE, annoyed, crosses over and opens it, revealing
    HANLON.*)

JOE. Oh, it's you. Come in, Sam.

HANLON. (*Enters, looks around.*) Where's the kid?

JOE. (*Startled.*) I thought you were going to pick her
up tomorrow.

HANLON. It's all Monty's fault.

JOE. Monty?

HANLON. My partner. He got pie-eyed last night on
our way to headquarters to check out. And when he's
pie-eyed, he talks too much. Did he spill the beans!

JOE. About Susan?

HANLON. And you and this whole setup! When the
Captain heard of it this morning, he hit the ceiling.

JOE. You can't take her away now. I don't have a
first-act curtain yet.

HANLON. The old man don't know from playwritin'.
He wants the kid brought in—today.

JOE. Are you going to let him ruin your first play?

HANLON. It's the play or me. (*Crossing toward bedroom.*) Don't tell me she's not up yet.

JOE. (JOE *races across room to stop him.*) Up and out.

HANLON. (*Startled.*) Out?

JOE. Out for breakfast. With Virgil.

    (*Waves* VIRGIL *back as he enters from kitchen.*)
Virgil took her out to breakfast.

HANLON. How come you didn't go along?

  JOE. I didn't feel like eating. My mind was too full of
the play. *Our* play.

HANLON. How long ago did they leave?

JOE. (*Crossing toward bedroom door.*) Oh, I'd say
Virgil and *Susan*—Susan, that is—I'd say they left
twenty minutes ago—*Sergeant Hanlon.*

HANLON. Sergeant Hanlon? Since when did you get so
formal with me?

JOE. As far as I'm concerned, it should be Lieutenant Hanlon. (*Starts moving him toward front door.*) Look, Lieutenant, why don't you drop back in an hour? She'll be here then for sure.

HANLON. I agree with you about the promotion— (*Pulls himself loose.*)—but they got Monty and me on the choppin' block. I got to take her in right away or I'll be wearin' my hat on my neck. (*Plops into chair Left of desk.*) I better wait here.

JOE. Sam, I'd be glad to have you wait. My home is your home—any time. But I'm expecting some friends, and—

HANLON. Always glad to meet your friends.

JOE. Not these. They're vulgar and obnoxious.

HANLON. They sound interestin'. I meet so many dull people in my racket.

(*The PHONE rings. JOE crosses to answer it.*)

JOE. Hello.—Oh, hello, Isabella! I forgot all about you. (*Listens.*) I mean—I can explain everything. Well—nearly everything.

(HANLON *rises and starts toward kitchen.* JOE *almost screams into phone.*)

Hold it, Isabella! (*Rushes over, stops* HANLON *just in time.*) What is it, Sam? You want something?

HANLON. What's all the excitement? I just want a cup of coffee. To steady my nerves.

JOE. (*Righteously indignant.*) Nobody waits on himself on Christmas Day in my house! (*Leads* HANLON *back to chair.*)

HANLON. I can get it and drink it before you're off the phone.

JOE. Do you want me to feel like a lousy host? (*Pushes him into chair, goes back to phone.*) Hello, Isabella. Now wait a minute—there's nothing to be upset about.

(*As* JOE *turns away with phone,* HANLON *gets up and starts for the kitchen again.*)

HANLON. Let's not be touchy about who gets the coffee.

JOE. (JOE *manages to catch* HANLON *by the arm.*)
Sam, you're a guest in my house! Sit down! Please!
    (HANLON *turns reluctantly, sits down, his back to*
    JOE.)
I'll get the coffee.

(*As he crosses to the kitchen door, it swings open and*
VIRGIL'S *arm comes out with a cup of coffee.* JOE
takes it, startled, and VIRGIL'S *arm disappears just*
as HANLON *turns around to say something.*)

HANLON. (*Reacting to sight of coffee, rises.*) That was
fast!

JOE. Oh, Virgil's got this place beautifully organized.
(*Hands him coffee.*) Sit down, Sam, and tell me all about
the police department.

HANLON. (*Sitting down.*) Well, there isn't much to
tell— (*Jumping up.*) I don't want to sit down! (*Starts
pacing with coffee, looks at it.*) Who the hell wants coffee? (*Puts down cup.*) I never should've brought that
kid up here. By the time the Captain gets through with
us, I'll be directing traffic in Long Beach.

JOE. He can't do that to you!

HANLON. Yeah? I'll wave to you when you drive by.
(*Looks at watch.*) How long does it take for 'em to eat?

JOE. Say—you could go down to the restaurant and
pick them up. Save a lot of time.

HANLON. Why didn't I think of that? Which joint is
it?

JOE. (*Guiding him by arm toward front door.*) A little
place I found. Out of this world. It's in Montebello.

HANLON. (*Stopping cold.*) Montebello! That's forty
miles from here!

JOE. I told you it was out of this world. You can use
the siren all the way and be there in no time.

HANLON. Montebello for one lousy meal?

JOE. The food's great. And confidentially, there's a

cute little waitress who works there. Virgil's got his eye on her.

HANLON. Virgil? I always figured he was a swish.

(*There is a CRASH of dishes in the kitchen.* JOE *and* HANLON *react and turn.*)

What the hell was that?

JOE. Isabella! I forgot all about her. (*Grabs phone, talks into it.*) Hello! Sorry I took so long, baby, but— (*Stops, reacts.*) She hung up.

HANLON. She really shook the joint doin' it.

JOE. You'd better hurry, Sam, or you'll miss them. (*Crosses to hurry him to front door.*)

HANLON. Yeah, yeah. What's the name of the joint?

JOE. The Shangri-La. On Whittier Boulevard. You drive straight down Wilshire—

HANLON. (*Interrupting.*) I know how to get there. You stick with the play, Joe, and if you didn't get enough out of the kid for three acts, make up some of it.

JOE. That's a crackerjack idea. (*Opening door.*) Sam, you're a credit to the department.

HANLON. I wish you'd tell that to the Captain. (*Plaintively.*) I hate Long Beach. (*Exits.*)

(JOE *closes the door and leans back against it, mopping his brow.* VIRGIL *enters from the kitchen, simultaneously with* SUSAN *from the bedroom. She wears a skirt and blouse, high-heeled shoes, and the rebosa.*)

VIRGIL. That dirty you-know-what! I ought to have him court-martialed!

JOE. What's with you?

VIRGIL. How many campaigns did I go through in the Pacific?

JOE. Seven.

VIRGIL. You know it was eight. How many nurses had a crush on me?

JOE. How could they resist a Lieutenant?

VIRGIL. And I had to go and fix him a cup of coffee! (*Looks at* SUSAN *as if he's seeing her for first time.*) I thought you were in Montebello.

SUSAN. (*Pirouetting.*) How do I look?

VIRGIL. Like jail bait.

JOE. You look fine. Go lose that rebosa and put your coat on. We're taking you out for Christmas dinner.

SUSAN. Okay, Joe. Anything you say. (*She exits into bedroom.*)

VIRGIL. (*Marveling.*) How do you do it?

JOE. Do what?

VIRGIL. Skip it.

JOE. You know the manager at the Shangri-La, don't you?

VIRGIL. I know everybody.

JOE. Phone him—tell him to tell Hanlon you left just before he got there.

VIRGIL. (*Indicating bedroom.*) What are you going to do about Junior?

JOE. Take her to dinner.

VIRGIL. I mean after dinner.

JOE. I haven't worked it out yet.

VIRGIL. Well, you'd better. (*Looking for match again.*) Don't you keep matches around here?

JOE. (*Pacing.*) I wish you could have heard her this morning, Virgil. She's got a lot of character for such a youngster.

VIRGIL. Youngster? In India her *daughter* would already be getting married. (*Lies down on couch.*)

JOE. They do things differently in— (*Stops, reacts.*) *That's it!*

VIRGIL. It is?

JOE. That Hindu girl and her daughter! We're going to the wedding.

VIRGIL. But I hardly know the people.

JOE. Virgil, I love you!

VIRGIL. And I was beginning to think it was Susan you were crazy about.

JOE. Don't be silly—I don't love her. But I'm going to marry her.

VIRGIL. (VIRGIL *sits up with a start.*) Marry her! Why?

JOE. (*Crossing to couch.*) As my wife—as anybody's wife—the law can't lay a hand on her. Can they?

VIRGIL. (*Rising.*) Joe, you're not serious?

JOE. Of course I'm serious.

VIRGIL. You're out of your mind! You're— (*Stops, heaves sigh of relief, relaxes.*) What am I running a fever for? You can't marry her. Ah! (*Spots lighter on desk. Lights cigarette.*) It works!

JOE. Why can't I marry her?

VIRGIL. A lot of reasons. One, she's under age. Two, there's a three-day law in this state.

JOE. Ever hear of Las Vegas?

VIRGIL. Who let Nevada into the Union?

JOE. After a couple of months, she can get an annulment.

VIRGIL. Won't that make juicy reading? (*Pretends to hold newspaper.*) "All Hollywood was startled today to hear of the sudden elopement of Joe Norton, one of our better known movie writers, and Susan Landis, seventeen-year-old debutante from Skid Row."

JOE. (*Waving him aside.*) That's not important.

VIRGIL. Only to your career.

JOE. It's not a marriage. It's an expedient.

VIRGIL. I won't be able to hold up my head in the Metro commissary.

JOE. That's life.

VIRGIL. You've forgotten just one little detail.

JOE. Like what?

VIRGIL. The bride. A girl with all that character might not want to—

(*He stops as* SUSAN *enters from bedroom. She wears the clothes she wore when* HANLON *brought her here.*)

JOE. All set?

SUSAN. I'm not going to dinner with you.

JOE. What are you talking about?

SUSAN. Nobody's going to marry me because I'm an expedient.

JOE. You weren't supposed to hear that.

SUSAN. When I get married it's going to be the biggest event of my life. A girl can marry the wrong guy any day in the week—but not this girl. (*Crossing toward front door.*) Goodbye—and thanks for everything.

JOE. You're not going anywhere!

SUSAN. (*Pushing him aside.*) That's what you think.

JOE. Virgil—call the airport and get two seats on the next plane to Vegas! (*Hurrying toward bedroom.*) Don't let her out of here. (*Exits.*)

VIRGIL. Get yourself another boy.

JOE. (*From bedroom.*) You heard what I said.

SUSAN. (*Low.*) Don't try to stop me, Virgil.

VIRGIL. (*Stepping out of her way.*) I never intended to. You're free, white and under twenty-one.

(SUSAN *exits just before* JOE *hurries in with topcoat.*)

JOE. Where's Susan?

VIRGIL. I don't know. I guess she had a previous engagement.

JOE. (*Crossing to open front door.*) Call the airport like I said. I'll be back sometime tonight. *Married.* (*Exits, closing door.*)

VIRGIL. I'm not calling anybody! (VIRGIL *looks after him, then walks to phone, sits on desk and dials. Into phone.*) Western Air lines? Have you got two tickets to Vegas on the next plane? Joe Norton. He'll be there in fifteen minutes.

(*Hangs up, concentrates on remembering another number, starts to dial.* MAIZEL *appears in doorway. He obviously has a hangover.*)

MAIZEL. (*Entering woozily.*) They told me Hanlon was here.

VIRGIL. He's having apoplexy on the road to Montebello.

MAIZEL. (*Indicates bar.*) How about a hair of the dog that bit me? Dog? I feel like a whole kennel got me.

VIRGIL. Help yourself. (*Finishes dialing as* MAIZEL *crosses to bar.*) Hello, Neil. You still legman for Louella? Good. Tell Louella that Joe wants her to be the first to know. He's getting married.

(MAIZEL *reacts, stops pouring in mid-air.*)

Tonight—Vegas. The bride? She's a debutante from Virginia. Susan Landis. You know—the *Virginia* Landises—the tobacco people. She's the beautiful tobacco heiress.

(MAIZEL *has walked over with drink in hand, now looks askance at it.*)

Yes, you might say it was a whirlwind courtship—

(MAIZEL *puts drink down, exits unsteadily.*)

CURTAIN

ACT TWO

SCENE 1

SCENE: *The same. It is the following morning.*

VIRGIL, *whistling "The Wedding March," is on the couch looking through a stack of newspapers. The room has been straightened up. There are fresh flowers around. Two open suitcases bulging with clothes are on the couch.* JOE *comes out of the bedroom with shirts and ties to put into the bags. The portable typewriter is in its carrying case on the desk.*

VIRGIL. Ah—the happy little bridegroom! Shall I pack your wedding certificate?

JOE. (*Packing.*) Don't forget my typewriter.

VIRGIL. Nothing like having a typewriter along on a honeymoon. How's the bride?

JOE. Sound asleep. Did you call Maude like I told you to?

VIRGIL. I call everybody like you tell me to. I'm Virgil, the human switchboard.

JOE. Oh, stop grousing. You know I can't take you on the honeymoon?

VIRGIL. You call this a honeymoon?

JOE. Would a raise make you any happier?

VIRGIL. Can you afford it with the extra mouth to feed?

JOE. Isn't a wife deductible?

VIRGIL. Not enough. What are you going to do about last week's love?

JOE. Isabella?

VIRGIL. The girl who gave you the best nights of her life.

JOE. I'll write her. Don't you worry about her. (*Hesitates.*) Any suggestions what to say?

VIRGIL. Washington's Farewell Address to his troops always plays.

GEORGETTE. (GEORGETTE *enters from kitchen.*) Good morning, Mr. Norton—Mr. Virgil. (*To* JOE.) Congratulations.

VIRGIL. Thanks.

GEORGETTE. I didn't mean you. (*Shaking her head negatively.*) Will you be staying for breakfast, Mr. Virgil?

VIRGIL. Stop shaking your head at me like that. I wasn't going to anyway.

GEORGETTE. I'll fix Mrs. Norton a nice breakfast. They tell me a bride gets pretty hungry the morning after. (*Exits into kitchen.*)

VIRGIL. (*Picking up a paper.*) Want to hear your obituary?

JOE. Is it any good ?

VIRGIL. All the world loves a lover. (*Reads.*) "All Hollywood except this columnist was taken by surprise today when Joe Norton, one of our better movie writers, eloped with Susan Landis, the eighteen-year-old heiress to the Landis tobacco fortune."

JOE. (*Closing suitcases.*) What were you drinking last night?

VIRGIL. (*Reads on.*) "I have been a friend of Susan's charming parents for more years than I care to admit. I remember with pleasure the many happy week-ends I spent on their Virginia *plantation?*" (*Picks up "Racing Form."*) Herb Stein in the *Racing Form* says "long-shot wins maiden race."

JOE. I'm all packed. You want to carry the typewriter?

VIRGIL. I still say—

JOE. (*Interrupting.*) —or would you rather carry the bags?

(VIRGIL *shrugs; crosses to desk and picks up the typewriter in its case.*)

VIRGIL. Some day you must tell me what really hap-
pened in Vegas.
   JOE. (*Picking up suitcases.*) You're not old enough.
   VIRGIL. Neither was the bride.

(*He opens the front door and they exit,* VIRGIL *closing
the door when he follows* JOE *out.*)

GEORGETTE. (*Entering from kitchen.*) Breakfast is
served. Shall I wake Mrs. Norton?
   (*Realizes they are gone. The PHONE rings and she
answers it.*)
Mr. Norton's residence. Good morning, Miss Isabella.
Merry Christmas! Isn't it the loveliest— (*Listens, aghast
at what she hears.*) Yes, ma'am. I'll tell him. (*Hangs
up.*) But not in those words. *No, ma'am!*

(*There is a KNOCK on the front door. She hurries to
answer it, opens door, reveals* HANLON *and* MAIZEL.
Each carries a bridal bouquet of flowers.)

HANLON. (*Offering bouquet.*) For the bride.
   MAIZEL. (*Offering his bouquet.*) For the groom.
   HANLON. (*Showing identical bouquets.*) We made a
package deal.
   GEORGETTE. Thank you. (*Following them as they enter
room.*) Would you mind telling me who you are?
   HANLON. We're the bridesmaids.
   MAIZEL. Pals of Mr. Norton. From the Vice Squad.
(*Crosses toward bedroom.*)
   GEORGETTE. Oh! You're the one who had a present for
him yesterday.
   HANLON. Sergeant Kris Kringle, that's me.
   GEORGETTE. Won't you sit down until he comes back?
   MAIZEL. (*Stops and turns.*) He ain't in the bedroom?

GEORGETTE. He *isn't* in the bedroom.

MAIZEL. Why ain't he?

GEORGETTE. I'm only the maid.

MAIZEL. (*Crossing to her.*) Come on, you can tell us, and we'll see that it goes easy for you downtown.

(*The PHONE rings.* GEORGETTE *crosses to answer it.*)

GEORGETTE. Mr. Norton's residence. Why, no, Miss Hopper, he isn't here. This is the maid. Just a moment, please. (*Holds hand over mouthpiece; to* COPS.) Hedda Hopper wants to know why she and Louella Parsons both had the same exclusive scoop.

MAIZEL. (*To* HANLON.) You're the writer.

HANLON. I ain't one of them ad lib writers. I got to dig for my material.

GEORGETTE. (*Into phone.*) I'm not sure, but I seem to remember Miss Landis told Mr. Norton her parents were going to phone Miss Parsons. Yes, I know they're old friends of yours, but it looks like they simply lost their heads— (*Listens for moment.*) Yes, I'll tell him you called. (*Hangs up, heaves sigh of relief.*)

HANLON. You been workin' for Joe long?

GEORGETTE. About a year. I met him when he gave a lecture on writing at U.C.L.A.

HANLON. You go to college or you just work there?

GEORGETTE. I'm a psychology major and I'm a Phi Beta Kappa. (*Exits into kitchen.*)

HANLON. Phi Beta Kappa?

MAIZEL. That's a colored fraternity. I met some of the boys.

(*There is a KNOCK on the door.*)

HANLON. (*In a whisper.*) Hey, I bet that's Joe and he forgot his key.

MAIZEL. Let's surprise him.

(*They hurry to stand on side of door as the KNOCK is*

repeated. GEORGETTE *enters from kitchen.* HANLON
*motions for her to open the door. She crosses to the
front door and pulls it wide open.* ISABELLA *barges
in. She is a most attractive dish in a smart suit,
mink stole and high heels.* HANLON *and* MAIZEL
pounce on her, pounding her back.)

HANLON. Joe, you old Sonofagun! } *(Simultaneously.)*
MAIZEL. Nice work, Joe!

(They draw back as they realize their mistake. ISABELLA
glares at them.)

ISABELLA. Do I look like Joe?

MAIZEL. *(Studying her charms.)* No Joe that I ever
knew.

GEORGETTE. May I take your wrap, Miss Isabella?

ISABELLA. I won't be staying that long. *(To* GEOR-
GETTE.) Friends of Joe's?

GEORGETTE. These gentlemen are from the Vice Squad.

ISABELLA. My favorite squad! *(Crossing to couch.)* Sit
down, boys, I want to talk to you.

MAIZEL. *(Follows her.)* It's a pleasure.

ISABELLA. Georgette, how about a cup of coffee? I
haven't slept a wink since I read the morning papers last
night.

GEORGETTE. Yes, ma'am.

ISABELLA. Where is he?

GEORGETTE. He'll be back in a minute. What did you
give Mr. Norton for Christmas?

ISABELLA. I haven't given it to him yet.

*(*GEORGETTE *exits.* ISABELLA *sits down, takes out cigarette.)*

MAIZEL. May I?

ISABELLA. May you what?

MAIZEL. *(Offering light.)* Light your cigarette.

ISABELLA. You're very sweet.

(*He lights her cigarette. She takes a long drag, then blows smoke into his face.*)

ISABELLA. (*Flaring up.*) Now listen, you two lame-brains—what's the idea of lousing up my life?

HANLON. What are you to Joe?

ISABELLA. You mean what *was* I?

MAIZEL. Yeah—what was you?

ISABELLA. Up to yesterday I was all he wanted out of life. For a wild, girlish moment, I even thought he was going to marry me. (*Picking up newspaper.*) Then this happens! How could he go for her?

MAIZEL. She's a Virginia tobacco heiress.

ISABELLA. Let's not be coy. She's a juvenile delinquent. A twelve-year-old nymphomaniac!

HANLON. She is not! She's seventeen.

ISABELLA. Nymphomania knows no age.

MAIZEL. What's with her, Sam?

HANLON. She's the woman scorned.

ISABELLA. Why did you have to bring her up here?

HANLON. Well, it was like this—Joe had this idea for—

(GEORGETTE *comes out of kitchen with a cup of coffee for* ISABELLA.)

ISABELLA. Thanks, Georgette. I really need this.

HANLON. You gonna hang around to see the man who got away?

ISABELLA. Yes. I like to stick pins into myself.

(*The DOORBELL rings.* GEORGETTE *crosses to the door and opens it.* MAUDE *stands there in a ski outfit, a pair of skis over one shoulder. She pushes the hood off her head so it rests on her back.*)

ISABELLA. Welcome to Sun Valley.

MAUDE. (*Entering.*) You're up early. (*Sees* HANLON *and* MAIZEL, *looks questioningly at* ISABELLA.) Friends of yours?

ISABELLA. Friend of Joe's. From the Vice Squad.

MAUDE. (*Sits in chair Right.*) Charmed.

HANLON. Likewise.

MAIZEL. I'm sure. (*To* HANLON.) Hey—this guy's got 'em all ages, ain't he?

ISABELLA. (*To* MAUDE.) They introduced Joe to the street waif he married yesterday in a moment of pity.

MAUDE. That was very nice of them. (*Reacts.*) Joe's married?

ISABELLA. Haven't you read the morning papers?

MAUDE. I never read with a hangover. Georgette! Quick, some coffee, please!

GEORGETTE. Yes, ma'am. Cream and sugar?

MAUDE. Just a little brandy.

(GEORGETTE *exits into kitchen.*)

ISABELLA. Why the ski clothes?

MAUDE. All I know is that I was lying in bed—alone, unfortunately—when the phone rang. It was Virgil.

MAIZEL. (*To* ISABELLA.) He's Joe's assistant.

MAUDE. Thanks loads. He tells me he's made an appointment for me at Magnin's. I go there and before I can open my mouth, I look like this!

HANLON. You sure ain't the type, lady, if anybody asks me.

MAUDE. Nobody asked you. (*To* ISABELLA.) My bags are packed and downstairs in the car. Virgil's supposed to meet me here and tell me who, what, where and why.

(*The bedroom door opens and* SUSAN *enters. She wears a suede Western skirt, a wide belt with a silver buckle, and a gaudily painted blouse. Obviously expensive, but also obviously Las Vegas.*)

SUSAN. (*Happily.*) How do I look, Joe? (*Realizes he isn't there.*) Where's Joe? I thought I heard his voice.

HANLON. All us writers talk alike.

MAIZEL. Hey—how does it feel to be married?

SUSAN. Wonderful. I don't know why I waited this long. (*Sees* ISABELLA. *Eyeing her.*) Do I know you?

ISABELLA. We're sort of related—through Joe. I'm Isabella.

SUSAN. Oh. We met on the phone, didn't we?

ISABELLA. Several times. (*Indicates* HANLON *and* MAIZEL.) I believe you've met your sponsors. (*Introducing* MAUDE.) And this is Joe's secretary, Maude— (*Hesitates.*) Do you have a last name, Maude?

MAUDE. (*Deadpan.*) Snodgrass.

SUSAN. Hello, Maude.

ISABELLA. She can tell you as much about Joe as I can. Only not the same kind of things.

MAUDE. Shut up, Isabella. (*Nicely, to* SUSAN.) Are you really Mrs. Norton?

ISABELLA. (*To* MAUDE.) Haven't you ever seen a wedding dress before?

SUSAN. (*Pirouetting.*) Joe bought me this in Las Vegas yesterday. What's wrong with it?

(GEORGETTE *enters with coffee for* MAUDE, *who crosses to bar and pours brandy into the coffee.*)

GEORGETTE. Good morning, Mrs. Norton. Isn't that the prettiest dress!

ISABELLA. It is if you like to do things on a horse.

GEORGETTE. I think it's lovely.

SUSAN. (*To* GEORGETTE.) Thank you—

GEORGETTE. —Georgette. Mr. Norton went downstairs.

SUSAN. Did he say when he was coming back?

GEORGETTE. No, ma'am. But if he stays away very long, he's crazy. I'll get your breakfast. (*Starts towards kitchen.*)

HANLON. How's the sandwich department in this cafeteria?

GEORGETTE. The icebox is all yours. (*Exits.*)

HANLON. How about you, Monty?

MAIZEL. I could eat.

HANLON. (*As they go.*) I wonder what caviar tastes like this time of the morning.

MAIZEL. (*Stopping to lean over* ISABELLA.) I'm a sucker for scorned women. Don't go away.

ISABELLA. Not a chance.

(MAIZEL *exits after* HANLON *into the kitchen.*)

MAUDE. (*Studying* SUSAN.) How old are you?

SUSAN. Seventeen.

MAUDE. That's a nice age to get married. I guess any age is a nice age to get married.

ISABELLA. (*To* SUSAN.) Was Joe sober last night?

SUSAN. He knew what he was doing.

ISABELLA. (*Rises, crosses to* SUSAN.) How long do you expect him to stay married to you?

SUSAN. All my life.

ISABELLA. Do you know how old he is?

SUSAN. Everybody knows how old Joe is. He's twenty-nine.

ISABELLA. Why do you think he married you?

SUSAN. Why don't you ask Joe that?

ISABELLA. I intend to.

MAUDE. Your claws are showing, Isabella.

ISABELLA. (*Turning to her.*) Why do *you* think he married her?

MAUDE. Could love have anything to do with it?

ISABELLA. Love! Do you know why Joe and I got along so well? Because that word never crept in between us.

SUSAN. Please get out of here.

ISABELLA. Maybe you think he married you because he couldn't live without you.

SUSAN. Are you going to leave?

ISABELLA. The thought hadn't occurred to me.

SUSAN. (*Crossing to kitchen door.*) Sergeant Hanlon!

ISABELLA. Why don't we just sit around and you ask me questions about Joe?

HANLON. (*Entering from kitchen with a sandwich.*) You call me?

(MAIZEL, *also eating a sandwich, enters after him.*)

MAIZEL. What's up?

SUSAN. Am I within my rights asking you to throw out someone who won't leave?

HANLON. If you're Mrs. Norton and this is Mr. Norton's home, you sure are.

MAIZEL. (*Crossing to* MAUDE.) What's this old bag been up to?

MAUDE. (*Indignantly.*) Me? I'm on *her* team.

MAIZEL. What position you playin'?

ISABELLA. *I'm* the fly in the ointment.

HANLON. Okay! According to Section 27, we gotta ask you to leave.

ISABELLA. (*Sits defiantly in chair.*) Nobody's going to throw me out of here.

HANLON. Nobody but us. (*To* MAUDE.) Hold my cheese sandwich. (*Hands it to her.*)

ISABELLA. You'll have to carry me out.

MAIZEL. Sounds fun. (*To* MAUDE.) Mine's ham. (*Hands sandwich to her.*)

ISABELLA. (*Folding her arms in defiance.*) You lay one finger on me and I'll have you broken!

MAIZEL. (*Approaching her.*) And I break so easy too.

HANLON. (*Following him.*) I'll take the legs, Monty.

MAIZEL. Oh, no, you don't!

(ISABELLA *starts to get up.* MAIZEL *tosses her over his shoulder and crosses to front door. It opens and* VIRGIL *enters.*)

VIRGIL. (*Startled.*) Isabella! What are you doing up there?

ISABELLA. It's my favorite position. (*Beating* MAIZEL *on back.*) Put me down, you ape.

MAIZEL. (*As he does.*) I think I ruptured my shoulder.

ISABELLA. It's been nice knowing you, Virgil. You and Joe both.

VIRGIL. He's writing you a letter.

ISABELLA. Tell him I don't live there any more.

(*Exits swinging her fur around her shoulders.* MAIZEL *starts after her.*)

HANLON. Where you goin'?

MAIZEL. I just remembered—I left the motor runnin'. (*Exits.*)

HANLON. (*Following him.*) I better go with— (*Stops, digs into pocket.*) How can that be? I got the key. (*Reacts, exits.*)

MAUDE. (*Slapping two sandwiches together.*) Anybody want a ham and cheese sandwich?

(SUSAN *takes the sandwich and exits into kitchen.*)

VIRGIL. Turn around. Let's see how you look.

MAUDE. (*Displaying her ski clothes.*) Will you explain this ridiculous getup to me?

VIRGIL. Joe borrowed Duke's cabin in the mountains.

(SUSAN *enters from kitchen in time to hear this.*)

MAUDE. Oh no—not again!

VIRGIL. He'll be waiting for you up there.

SUSAN. You mean he'll be waiting for me, don't you?

VIRGIL. (*Turning to her.*) No, I don't mean that at all. He'll be up there for weeks—maybe months. You'll be down here.

MAUDE. What kind of marriage is that?

VIRGIL. Joe's going to be busy writing a play.

SUSAN. What play?

VIRGIL. He says it's all about you and your mother, who wanted love.

SUSAN. That's all *I* want.

MAUDE. That makes two of us.

SUSAN. Why can't he write the play here?

VIRGIL. Because he'd be concentrating on you.

MAUDE. What's wrong with that?

VIRGIL. Everything. Joe's not in love with her.

SUSAN. Do you know why Joe married me?

VIRGIL. Of course I know. To keep you from being sent away to—

SUSAN. (*Interrupting.*) Because he needed me. Just like I told him he did.

VIRGIL. He lied. To get you to go through with the marriage.

SUSAN. (*Hurt.*) He lied to me?

VIRGIL. To save you from the prison farm. You'll probably never see him again.

SUSAN. But he's my husband. He can't do this to me. Why, last night he told me—

(*She suddenly breaks, runs into bedroom, closing door. GEORGETTE enters from kitchen with breakfast tray.*)

GEORGETTE. Here's your breakfast, Mrs. Norton.

MAUDE. I don't think Mrs. Norton's very hungry.

GEORGETTE. Oh! Something wrong?

MAUDE. Yeah. Put the eggs back in the shells.

GEORGETTE. Okay. (*Exits into kitchen.*)

VIRGIL. (*Indicating bedroom as he crosses to bar.*) What the hell's the matter with her?

MAUDE. I could kick you in the teeth.

VIRGIL. (*Turning with bottle and glass.*) Why? She didn't let me tell her the *good* news.

MAUDE. Such as?

VIRGIL. Such as Joe's going to send her to a dramatic coach.

MAUDE. Now isn't that a dandy wedding present!

VIRGIL. She'll have six lessons a week. We're going to make an actress out of her.

MAUDE. Why?

VIRGIL. When Joe writes this play, he wants her to go to New York and try for the part of the girl. He thinks she's got talent.

MAUDE. That's all very well, except for one thing.

VIRGIL. What's that?

MAUDE. No play.

VIRGIL. (*Crossing to her with bottle and drink.*) He'll write this one.

MAUDE. Stop kidding old Maude, will you? You know the routine as well as I do. (*Taking glass before it can reach his lips.*) I know you don't like to drink alone.

VIRGIL. This play means something to him.

MAUDE. So did the last three he started. (*Downs drink, shudders.*) If liquor only tasted like orange juice!

VIRGIL. This play's different, Maude. I don't know how she did it—or why the story of Susan and her mother hit him so hard—but I think he's back on the beam.

MAUDE. Yeah? Two weeks from now he won't remember what Susan looks like or anything she said about her mother.

VIRGIL. He'll come through this time. He's got to—or he's dead. (*Crosses to bar with bottle.*)

(SUSAN *enters slowly from the bedroom. Again she wears her own clothes. The* OTHERS *are not aware of her presence as* VIRGIL *pours himself a drink.*)

MAUDE. If he's dead, so are you, Virgil.

VIRGIL. Now what does that mean?

MAUDE. You know damn well what it means.

VIRGIL. Don't tell me.

SUSAN. I'll tell him.

(*They turn and see her.*)

VIRGIL. Good God! Raggedy Ann is here again! Don't you ever get tired of that routine?

SUSAN. I'm tired of being pushed around. But I guess you're not.

VIRGIL. Nobody pushes me around! (*Indicating sleeve.*) Not since I got my stripes. (*Reacts.*)

SUSAN. (*Crossing to* VIRGIL.) You haven't any idea how sorry Joe is for you, have you?

VIRGIL. Joe sorry for me? Why, he was only a seaman first-class.

SUSAN. Why do you think Joe has you around? You and your college education and your Navy rank and your crew haircut.

VIRGIL. I earn my keep.

SUSAN. In a job he made up for you! You were his commanding officer—a guy with rank. But I say Joe pushes you around every time he gives you a helping hand. He's your crutch—and you're not man enough to walk without it.

MAUDE. I've been saying the same thing for months, but not half as well.

VIRGIL. I think you've both said enough. (*To* SUSAN.) Now *I've* got something to say to you. Joe wants to make an actress out of you.

SUSAN. I don't want to be an actress. I want to be a wife. Last night Joe told me I was the most wonderful girl in the whole world. (*At silence from* OTHERS.) He meant it! I know he did! (*She exits hurriedly into kitchen.*)

MAUDE. I like crimes that pay.

VIRGIL. (*Takes out notebook, looks at it, checks off items.*) His lawyer's cleared everything with the State authorities. Nobody'll bother her any more.

MAUDE. Just her dramatic coach.

VIRGIL. She'll live here until the tryouts in New York.

MAUDE. First he's got to write the play. Put that in your little notebook.

VIRGIL. (*Looking at notes again.*) Tomorrow I'll see

about the annulment, but we won't put that through for
a couple of months yet.

MAUDE. To keep the pain alive a little longer?

VIRGIL. Until the publicity in the papers dies down.
    (SUSAN, *wearing her old hat and coat, enters from
    kitchen, starts for front door.*)
Where do you think you're going?

SUSAN. You can send the annulment papers to me care
of General Delivery.

VIRGIL. (*Frantic.*) You can't go! Joe'll fire me if I let
you get away!

MAUDE. Your own shipmate would do that to you?

(VIRGIL *gives her a dirty look. The PHONE rings. He
                walks over to answer it.*)

VIRGIL. (*Into phone.*) Hello. Joe?
    (SUSAN *stops in doorway.*)
Where are you? (*To* OTHERS.) Good God! He's stuck in
Cucamonga! (*Listens for a moment; angrily.*) The Cadillac broke down again? Put it in reverse and let it roll
down the mountain! (*Pause.*) Where are you exactly?
Okay—I'll have Maude pick you up in her car. Of
course she'll be up there. She's got to eat, doesn't she?

MAUDE. I don't know why.

SUSAN. (*Crossing to phone.*) I want to talk to him.

VIRGIL. (*Waves her aside.*) It's no sale on Susan. She's
leaving. (*After a pause.*) She wants no part of being an
actress or taking dramatic lessons.

SUSAN. (*Takes phone from him.*) All I want is you,
Joe. (*Listens for a moment.*) Were you lying to me last
night? Were you? You can tell me. I'm a big girl now.
(*She listens, tears come to her eyes.*) Okay, Joe. Anything you say. I'll work hard. Goodbye. (*She hangs up,
starts to take off her coat as she crosses toward bedroom
and exits.*)

VIRGIL. Will you please tell me why women cry when
they're happy?

MAUDE. I wouldn't know. I've never been that happy. He lied to her again, didn't he?

VIRGIL. (*Defensively.*) He had to. It was for her own good.

MAUDE. Men! Whenever they hurt a woman, it's always for her own good. (*Crossing room.*) Give me my skis! (*Grabbing them from* VIRGIL *as he picks them up.*) I hope I break two legs—and both of them are Joe's!

(*She exits.* VIRGIL *looks after her.*)

CURTAIN

ACT TWO

SCENE 2

SCENE: *The same. It is nearly three months later.*

VIRGIL *is at the desk, talking on the phone.* GEORGETTE *is sitting on the couch, doing schoolwork on the coffee table.*

VIRGIL. (*Into phone.*) What's the difference why? Just cut through the red tape, will you, Mac? It's been months. (*Listens momentarily.*) Of course I'm serious. It's my life, isn't it? Okay. Goodbye. (*Hangs up, turns to* GEORGETTE.) You didn't hear a word I said.

GEORGETTE. I didn't even know you were on the phone.

VIRGIL. Smart girl.

GEORGETTE. Not today I'm not. Spring exams start tomorrow.

VIRGIL. Oh, you'll pass.

GEORGETTE. I'm talking about Ralph. This is his paper on music appreciation.

VIRGIL. Music appreciation? That was the big pipe course at Yale.

GEORGETTE. It's the big pipe course everywhere. That's why Professor Schmidt is so furious.

VIRGIL. If Ralph flunks, he can't play football next fall, can he?

GEORGETTE. Oh, he won't flunk. In fourteen years nobody's failed the course, and Professor Schmidt says nobody as stupid as Ralph is going to ruin his record.

VIRGIL. We all have our little problems.

GEORGETTE. What's yours?

VIRGIL. Lillian wants to get married.

GEORGETTE. To you?

VIRGIL. Good God no! She makes three times as much money as I do. She's met a guy who makes three times as much as *she* does.

GEORGETTE. What did you tell her?

VIRGIL. To ask him if he could find a rich girl for me. (*The PHONE rings. VIRGIL answers it.*)

(*Into phone.*) Hello. What are you and Joe doing in town? Did you bring me down some snowballs like I told you to? (*Listens for a moment.*) Yeah—Susan'll be checking in here any minute. Oh, we're great friends now. Cry on each other's shoulders like mad. Say—who writes those letters to the kid—you or Joe? I sure hope the play's better than they are. Hurry over—I'll light a bottle of bourbon for you in the window. (*Hangs up.*)

GEORGETTE. Shall I hide the liquor or wasn't that Miss Maude?

VIRGIL. It was and don't.

GEORGETTE. How is she?

VIRGIL. Still a strain on her girdle.

GEORGETTE. It'll be nice to see Mr. Norton again.

VIRGIL. Oh—he won't be coming over here. Doesn't want to run into you know who.

GEORGETTE. (*Cynically.*) He's really a loving husband.

VIRGIL. Sex does not a marriage make.

GEORGETTE. Neither do dramatic lessons. (*Crosses to kitchen.*) Can I fix you a sandwich?

VIRGIL. Sure. What have we got in the house?

GEORGETTE. Nothing.

VIRGIL. Okay. Make mine on white toast. I need the energy.

GEORGETTE. You know, Mr. Virgil, I think I'll write my Master's thesis about you. (*Exits into kitchen.*)

VIRGIL. You do and I'll sue every initial in U.C.L.A.

(*The front door opens and* SUSAN *enters. She is trim, neat, pert in a Spring dress.*)

SUSAN. Hi, sailor boy.

VIRGIL. Doesn't anybody ever knock on a door around here? I might have been—

SUSAN. Not you. Yale men are never caught in embarrassing situations.

VIRGIL. That's Harvard men you're thinking of. They're never caught in anything. And stop growing up so fast.

SUSAN. I *have* to grow up fast. To catch up with my husband.

VIRGIL. How many times do I have to tell you Joe's your husband in name only. And not even that for much longer.

SUSAN. I want to hear it from Joe.

VIRGIL. Will you give up then?

SUSAN. No. Where's Georgette?

VIRGIL. Fixing me an ice cube sandwich.

SUSAN. Sounds good. (*Calling into kitchen.*) Hi, Georgette! Surprise me with something.

(*She sits down on the couch and starts to tamp a cigarette, but crushes it on her wrist. She quickly lights another one, puffs on it amateurishly.* VIRGIL *crosses over to her, fascinated.*)

VIRGIL. What do you think you're doing?

SUSAN. Smoking. This is a cigarette. Sir Walter Raleigh discovered the Indians doing this in the year—

VIRGIL. You don't smoke.

SUSAN. I do now. Makes me look older. Will you teach me to make smoke rings?

VIRGIL. (*Sits beside her.*) No. And stop pretending you're so grown up.

SUSAN. I can pretend to be anything. According to my dramatic coach. (*She puts out the cigarette in an ash-tray on the coffee table, banging it a good dozen times before she lets it go.*)

VIRGIL. (*Finally.*) Are you sure it's dead?

(*She nods.*)

How are your dramatic lessons going?

SUSAN. Today Mr. Stanislawsky taught me how to be a bridge chair. Tomorrow I'm going to be a table top with a checkered cloth.

VIRGIL. Remind me to stop payment on his last check.

SUSAN. You should. They knew more about dramatics at Eagle Rock High. We carried our books under our arms there. This guy wants 'em on your head. (*Puts book on head.*) Get this big deal! (*Walks gingerly across room.*) What am I?

VIRGIL. (*After snapping fingers.*) Don't tell me. (*Finally.*) A girl with a book on her head.

SUSAN. Say, you're bright.

VIRGIL. It's nothing, really.

SUSAN. And those phoney terms he uses! (*Demonstrates with her arms as she talks.*) Compression! Dynamics! Dynamics! Compression!

VIRGIL. What are you supposed to be now—a Thunderbird engine?

SUSAN. I think Joe's throwing our money away.

VIRGIL. Our money?

SUSAN. Someone told me about community property yesterday. (*Crosses back to couch and sits beside him.*) Are we very rich?

VIRGIL. We're loaded.

SUSAN. How do I get my hands on some of it?

VIRGIL. What do you want money for? Aren't your bills all paid?

SUSAN. I found out I can take a bus to Snowtop Lodge for $11.67.

VIRGIL. That's exactly why you're never allowed more than ten dollars in cash at one time.

SUSAN. A girl's entitled to make a pass at her husband once in a while.

VIRGIL. When he finishes the play.

SUSAN. When will he finish the play?

VIRGIL. You know as much about it as I do.

(GEORGETTE *enters with a sandwich on a plate.*)
It's about time.

GEORGETTE. Hello, Miss Susan.

SUSAN. (*With a grin.*) Can't you ever remember it's Mrs. Norton?

GEORGETTE. (*Crossing to couch.*) Not till Mr. Norton does.

SUSAN. We women sure think alike, don't we?

GEORGETTE. (*Putting down sandwiches.*) We have to. (*Exits into kitchen.*)

SUSAN. I went to the library today. What do you think I read?

VIRGIL. A book?

SUSAN. "What Every Married Woman Should Know."

VIRGIL. A smart author would get rich with a book called "What Every Married Woman *Shouldn't* Know." (*Takes bite of sandwich, reacts.*) Salami! What a comedown!

SUSAN. (*Taking sandwich from him.*) I'll eat it.

(*There is a KNOCK on the door.*)

VIRGIL. If I know that knock, Maude's here. (*Calling off.*) Come in, bachelor girl.

(*The door opens and* MAUDE *enters.* SUSAN *and* VIRGIL *cross over to greet her.*)

SUSAN. Hi, Maude! (*Parades with book on her head.*) Look—I'm an actress.

MAUDE. Are you sure that's how Audrey Hepburn started?

SUSAN. And I can smoke cigarettes now.

MAUDE. By yourself?

(VIRGIL *helps her off with her coat.*)

VIRGIL. Make like a Thunderbird for Maude. With the top down, this time.

SUSAN. (*Going into act.*) Dynamics! Compression! Compression! Dynamics!

MAUDE. Okay. Put the top up.

SUSAN. My teacher says he's never seen such acting.

MAUDE. I don't believe I have either. Let me look at you, Susan. (*She pirouettes.*) Nice. How are you?

SUSAN. Older. I won't ask you how Joe is, because everybody answers me like I'm a child.

MAUDE. (*Sits on couch and takes off gloves.*) He's just fine, child.

VIRGIL. Doesn't he ever hunger for the gentle touch of a woman's loving hand?

MAUDE. He's got *me*.

VIRGIL. Answer the question. The druggist told me the doctor told him that Joe sent down for some more sleeping pills. Why?

MAUDE. He made friends with a bear who's got insomnia. Has a lot of trouble hibernating.

VIRGIL. The bear or Joe?

MAUDE. I wouldn't know—I've got my own room.

VIRGIL. (*Crossing to put coat on chair.*) Have you read any of the play or are you just typing it?

MAUDE. I thought the first two acts were wonderful.

SUSAN. (*Eagerly, sitting beside her.*) He's got two acts already?

MAUDE. He *had* two acts already.

VIRGIL. How did you burn the pages this time?

MAUDE. On a flaming stick—like shish kabob.

SUSAN. (*Aghast at thought.*) You burned Joe's writing?

MAUDE. It seemed the merciful thing to do.

SUSAN. What was wrong with it? (*Rises, poses.*) I've had a very dramatic life.

MAUDE. Your mother kept getting in the way.

SUSAN. My mother? What's she doing in *my* play?

MAUDE. Lousing it up.

VIRGIL. Has he started page 1, scene 1 again?

MAUDE. He will as soon as he cleans up this income tax mess.

VIRGIL. What's the matter?

MAUDE. The government won't let him deduct you as a dependent.

(*The PHONE rings. MAUDE catches VIRGIL by the arm as he starts for it.*)

Gee, can I answer it? We're so far up in the snow country that—

VIRGIL. (*With a gesture.*) Go ahead. Live a little.

MAUDE. (*Crossing to PHONE as it rings again.*) Hello. (*Reacts, puts hand over receiver.*) There's someone on the other end! (*Into phone.*) No, he isn't, Mr. Winfield. Did he tell you he'd be here? (*Listens.*) How does it look on the income tax deal? Oh? Yes, I'll tell him. 'Bye. (*Hangs up.*)

VIRGIL. (*With nod toward SUSAN.*) Joe's coming over here?

MAUDE. For a few minutes. He needs some papers to prove he spent some money that he didn't.

SUSAN. (*Rises quickly and starts for bedroom.*) I better get dressed up. I know just what to wear.

VIRGIL. (*Catching her by arm.*) You'd better get out of here.

SUSAN. (*Pulling away.*) I've got a better idea. Why don't you two get out and leave me here with Joe?

VIRGIL. Joe doesn't want to see you, Susan. Take a walk down to the ocean. It's only seven miles.

SUSAN. I've seen the ocean. I haven't seen Joe. (*Exits into bedroom.*)

VIRGIL. (*Turning to* MAUDE.) Now what do we do?

MAUDE. Well—I could run down the road and warn him by waving a red lantern. Like this! (*Demonstrates.*) The bridge is out! Stop the train! Stop, engineer, stop before it's too late!

(JOE, *carrying a briefcase, enters as* MAUDE *is waving. He surveys her with surprise.*)

JOE. What's the matter with you?

MAUDE. I'm a freight train with the top down.

JOE. (*Coming further into room.*) Hello, Virgil. What's new?

VIRGIL. I wish I'd said that.

JOE. (*Looking around, drops briefcase on desk.*) Place looks the same.

VIRGIL. (*Pointedly.*) There's a new addition in the bedroom.

JOE. We always needed another closet. How did it work out?

MAUDE. It's learned to smoke cigarettes.

JOE. (*Giving her dubious look.*) We must've come down from the mountains too fast. Have you got the bends?

SUSAN. (SUSAN *enters from bedroom during above. She is smoking a cigarette in a holder.*) She means me.

JOE. (JOE *turns to study her as she walks in dramatically, then faces* MAUDE *and* VIRGIL.) Did you two frame this?

SUSAN. No—they asked me to leave before you got here. How long are you going to be in town?

JOE. (*Crossing toward bedroom.*) Not long enough. Do you mind if I get some of my papers?

SUSAN. Help yourself.

(JOE *gives her a look and exits into bedroom.*)

MAUDE. (*To* VIRGIL.) Wouldn't you like to show me how the petunias are doing this year?

VIRGIL. It's too early for petunias.

MAUDE. (MAUDE *crosses and takes him firmly by the arm.*) Well then, let's find the first Spring robin and wring his little neck.

VIRGIL. Oh—a fellow bird lover!

(*They cross toward front door.*)

MAUDE. (*At door.*) Give you five minutes with him, Susan. After that I might lose my job.

SUSAN. Thanks.

VIRGIL. (*To* MAUDE.) Shall we go, Mrs. Audubon?

(*They exit, closing the door.* SUSAN *crosses to the couch and lies down dreamily. After a beat,* JOE *enters from the bedroom with a sheaf of papers, crosses to the phone without noticing* SUSAN. *He sits down, dials hurriedly.* SUSAN *pulls her skirt up over one knee, but* JOE *is so busy putting the papers into his briefcase with his free hand that he misses this action.* SUSAN *sighs and drops one shoulder strap of her dress.*)

JOE. (*Into phone.*) Hello—George? Pull your skirt down and put that strap back on your shoulder!

(SUSAN *reacts, sits up.*)

(*Into phone.*) I didn't mean you, George. I found the records. I'll drop 'em off at the office before I go back to the mountains. Okay. (*Hangs up.*)

SUSAN. (*Rising.*) Do you have to go back?

JOE. I work better up there.

(*He crosses to the bar and* SUSAN *follows him.*)

SUSAN. Is that why you tore up the first two acts?

JOE. (*Pouring a drink.*) How's your acting?

SUSAN. As bad as your writing.

JOE. Aren't you learning anything?

SUSAN. Don't worry. I'll be a finished actress by the time your play's finished.

JOE. By then they'll cast you for the part of your mother.

SUSAN. (*As he starts to drink.*) How about a cup of coffee instead of that?

JOE. I don't know. The last time I drank some of your coffee, I wound up married.

SUSAN. So did I.

JOE. I'll settle for a cup of weak tea.

SUSAN. Okay. But I warn you—it'll taste like coffee. (*Exits into kitchen.*)

SUSAN. (*Off.*) What are you doing to my mother in the play?

JOE. What's she doing to *me?*

SUSAN. (*Off.*) You don't understand *her* any better than you do me.

JOE. I don't even understand myself.

SUSAN. (*Entering with coffee.*) I feel terribly mistreated.

JOE. (*Crosses to couch and sits.*) Why? I haven't done so badly by you.

SUSAN. (*Giving him coffee and sitting on arm of couch.*) You haven't? Look—a woman would rather be slapped in the face and drug around by the hair—as long as her man's around—

JOE. (*Moving away from her.*) I'm not your man and you're not a woman. (*Sips coffee.*) You made better coffee before you pretended to be grown up. This is terrible!

SUSAN. Georgette made it.

JOE. Oh! It's pretty good—after the first sip.

SUSAN. (*Sliding onto couch beside him.*) Now—about the play. What's your problem?

JOE. (*Rises and moves away from her to armchair Right.*) You're going to solve it?

SUSAN. (*Following him.*) It's my responsibility. Every wife should be interested in her husband's career.

JOE. Stop referring to yourself as my wife!

SUSAN. Okay, okay—I was an expedient. Now—what kind of love story are you writing?

JOE. It's not a love story. It's an exposé of juvenile delinquency.

SUSAN. (*Shocked.*) You're not writing about Mom or me as a great love story?

JOE. (*Moving away from her to bar again.*) Where's the great love story in a mother who runs off with a man and deserts a young daughter who has to get married to stay out of jail?

SUSAN. (*Following him.*) You writers certainly make things sound dull.

JOE. Did you ever write a play?

SUSAN. I lived one. You're just not smart enough to put it on paper.

JOE. Miss Landis—

SUSAN. Mrs. Norton.

JOE. Mrs. Norton—

SUSAN. Susan.

JOE. Okay. Susan. (*Turning to her.*) Can you stand one more week of dramatic lessons?

SUSAN. Why?

JOE. Because I can stand just one more week of that snow country. If the play doesn't jell by then, I'd like my house and my name back.

SUSAN. And my signature on those silly annulment papers?

JOE. That's right.

SUSAN. (SUSAN *turns away from him and crosses to couch. Sitting.*) Would you be mad if I started to cry right now?

JOE. (*Pouring himself a drink.*) Real tears or dramatic-school tears?

SUSAN. You know something, Mr. Norton?

JOE. Joe.

SUSAN. Okay. Joe. You're not important enough for me to cry over.

(*He stops pouring.*)

I used to be interested in you as a man—as the guy I loved—but not now.

JOE. (*Surprised.*) No?

SUSAN. (*Rises, crosses to him.*) No. All I want out of you is a good play so I can be a good actress—if it's in me to be one. But mostly, I don't want to let my mother down.

JOE. How did we get back to her?

SUSAN. She and *her* Joe are saving every penny to come to New York for the opening. After she has the baby.

JOE. Your mother's going to be a mother?

SUSAN. *Her* husband knows how to be a husband. I'll read you her last letter. (*Crosses to desk.*) It's around here someplace. (*Finds letter.*) Here it is. I saved the stamps, like you told me to. (*Indicating couch.*) Sit down.

(JOE *crosses to couch, eyeing her doubtfully.*)

Stop looking at me like I'm Lizzie Borden. (*As he hesitates.*) Sit down.

(JOE *sits.*)

(*Reads from letter.*) "Dearest Susan: You've made me the happiest woman on this side of the Andes. Imagine you married to the best writer in the whole world." (*To* JOE.) I exaggerated slightly.

JOE. Slightly.

SUSAN. (*Reading again.*) "One thing bothers me, though. If you're so much in love with Joe, why are you spending all your time with this fellow Virgil? The sun is very hot here in Peru—but it doesn't sound right to me." (*To* JOE.) Does it sound right to you?

JOE. Keep reading.

SUSAN. (*Reading again.*) "I want you to be the first to know I'm going to have a baby."

JOE. She'll have to tell her husband sometime.

SUSAN. (*Sits in chair, continues reading.*) "I feel it

will be the beginning of a new life for me. After all the
lives I've led. First when I was a kid in Texas. Then
when I met your father and we were married. And after
you were born. And when your father *left* me. It's amazing how many people don't realize they live so many
lives—not just one. Why, when I was—"

JOE. (*Interrupting, rises.*) Wait a minute! Read that
last part again.

SUSAN. "It's amazing how many people don't realize
they live so many lives?"

JOE. (*Excited.*) That's it! Kiss your mother for me—
when you see her in New York!

SUSAN. (*Rising to face him.*) I could do with a little
kissing myself.

JOE. (*Taking letter from her and reading through it.*)
Susan, your mother's a better playwright than both of
us.

SUSAN. Mom's a playwright?

JOE. She's the new Lillian Hellman. (*Pacing.*) "Five
Lives"—that's what I'll call it—the five lives of a woman
before she becomes a woman. Now I think we're going
to have a play!

SUSAN. (*Eagerly.*) When do we leave for the mountains?

JOE. (*Returning letter to her.*) No we—*me*. You stay
here. Keep studying—and keep writing your mother—
like a good daughter.

SUSAN. (*Enthusiasm fading.*) If that's the way you
want it, Joe.

JOE. That's the way. (*Crossing to get his briefcase on
desk.*) Oh—and sign those annulment papers. No point
in being silly about them, is there? (*Crosses to front
door, turns as she doesn't answer.*) Is there?

SUSAN. No point at all.

JOE. That's a sensible girl. (*Exits.*)

SUSAN. (SUSAN *walks to desk, looks at letter in her
hand.*) He might have stayed here and found out he

liked me. But you had to go and give him an idea! I
hope your new baby looks like—like me!

(*The front door opens.* VIRGIL *enters.*)

VIRGIL. What happened? Joe just grabbed Maude and
said he had work to do in the mountains.
SUSAN. What would you do if your husband fell head
over heels for another woman?
VIRGIL. Anyone we know?
SUSAN. My mother. Lillian Hellman!
VIRGIL. (VIRGIL *picks up cigarette* SUSAN *tamped out,
sniffs it suspiciously.*) Hey, what were you smoking?

CURTAIN

ACT TWO

SCENE 3

SCENE: *An afternoon in October.*

MAUDE *is seated at the desk. She is busy clipping reviews from New York newspapers and gluing them
into a large scrapbook.*

GEORGETTE, *an open hatbox beside her, is trying on a
new hat in front of the mirror.*

GEORGETTE. How does it look, Miss Maude?
MAUDE. Terrific. Where'd you get it?
GEORGETTE. It's a copy of a Christian Dior model—
from Ohrbach's. You like it?
MAUDE. Don't ask me. I haven't worn a hat since I
came to California.
GEORGETTE. That's a lot of years, isn't it?
MAUDE. Let's not be specific. I remember I drove out

here in a model T with a girl friend. She was going to sweep Wally Reid off his feet and I had my cap set for Richard Dix. (*Sighs.*) He never knew. How would you like to pour me a short one?

GEORGETTE. (*Crossing to bar.*) This has become the drinkinest house.

MAUDE. I only drink to forget. The trouble is that by the time I get tight, I can't remember what I'm trying to forget. (*Putting thought aside.*) How's school this year?

GEORGETTE. (*Pouring drink.*) Couldn't be better. Ralph just got a scholarship.

MAUDE. I thought he made such bad grades.

GEORGETTE. He does, but he also made two touchdowns against Oregon State last Saturday.

MAUDE. Sounds like quite a student.

(GEORGETTE *crosses to* MAUDE *with the drink.*)

To Brooks Atkinson! Love that man!

GEORGETTE. How many stars did he give the play?

MAUDE. He doesn't give stars. He makes them. (*Downs drink, picks up the "New Yorker," turns to the review.*)

GEORGETTE. (*During above.*) It's a funny thing. When I first saw Miss Susan, I thought she was rich. Now it turns out she's talented. Which is better?

(MAUDE *scans the "New Yorker" review, drops the magazine distastefully into the wastebasket.*)

The *New Yorker* didn't like it?

MAUDE. They didn't understand it. Over their heads.

GEORGETTE. Don't they like anything?

MAUDE. Only dirty, foreign movies.

GEORGETTE. How did George Jean Nathan like the play?

MAUDE. (*Finds his notice.*) From his review I can't tell if he saw it or not. All he talks about is Susan.

GEORGETTE. Some men have a weakness for eighteen-year-olds.

MAUDE. All men have. Only he admits it. (*Reads from notice.*) "Last night a new star was born who may some day rank with the greats of the theatre—" (*Mumbles next words.*) "—nymphlike quality—young, eager Susan Landis, new darling of Broadway—" I think I'll press this between two roses.

GEORGETTE. Isn't that nice?

MAUDE. Can you imagine being so happy at eighteen? (*An afterthought.*) Can you imagine being eighteen?

GEORGETTE. Why, you don't look a day over—(*Hesitates.*)—you don't!

MAUDE. Okay.

GEORGETTE. Tell me something. If Miss Susan is so happy, why is Mr. Norton so unhappy? He wrote a hit show, didn't he?

MAUDE. Success isn't everything. I think that's a line from any Clifford Odets play.

(*There is a KNOCK on the door.* GEORGETTE *crosses and opens it, revealing* VIRGIL. *He wears a smart trench-coat and carries a plaid valet pack.*)

VIRGIL. (*Entering.*) The prodigal returns! Put a light under the fatted calf.

GEORGETTE. Welcome home, Mr. Virgil. How was New York?

VIRGIL. People say it's just like San Francisco, but I can't see it.

MAUDE. I hate to say it, but it's good to have you back.

VIRGIL. (*Putting down luggage.*) Where's Joe? He didn't meet me at the airport.

MAUDE. He met you. Three days ago.

VIRGIL. The fog was so thick we landed at Burbank.

GEORGETTE. Now, Mr. Virgil, you know that didn't hold you up for three days.

VIRGIL. (*Crossing to bar.*) I stopped over in Washington.

MAUDE. Bring me a spare. Tell us all about the play.

VIRGIL. (*As he fixes drinks for himself and* MAUDE.) I saw it six times.

MAUDE. That's six times more than the author did.

GEORGETTE. Why didn't Mr. Norton go East for rehearsals or anything?

VIRGIL. He was afraid he'd like the play.

MAUDE. He was afraid he'd like Susan.

VIRGIL. (*Crossing to her with drinks.*) How's Joe feeling?

MAUDE. Lousy might be a good word for it. He's worse now than he was before you left.

VIRGIL. Didn't the reviews cheer him up?

MAUDE. Go out in the kitchen and count the empties.

VIRGIL. What happened to his psychiatrist?

MAUDE. He's had a breakdown. (*Toasting with glass.*) Well, cheers!

(*There is a KNOCK on the door.*)

HANLON. (*Off.*) Open up! It's the police.
MAIZEL. (*Off.*) No, it ain't. It's us.

(GEORGETTE *crosses and opens the door.* HANLON *and* MAIZEL *enter. They are dressed to kill.* MAIZEL *heads directly for bar.*)

MAUDE. Abbott and Costello!

VIRGIL. To what do we owe this dubious pleasure?

HANLON. (*Taking center stage.*) We couldn't leave town without sayin' goodbye to our friends. Monty and me are goin' to New York.

MAIZEL. It'll be the first time I been east of Azusa.

MAUDE. Aren't you nervous?

MAIZEL. What's to be nervous? My wife ain't goin'.

GEORGETTE. (*Crossing to kitchen.*) Excuse me—I'll get some ice.

MAIZEL. (*Face lighting up.*) Ice like in highballs?

HANLON. Control yourself, Monty.

(GEORGETTE *exits.*)

VIRGIL. I see you've been transferred to the Plain-clothes Squad. What's the occasion?

HANLON. What's the occasion he asks! We finagled ourselves a two-week vacation.

MAIZEL. Blew the bankroll for this trip.

HANLON. Sure. We didn't want Susan to be ashamed of us.

MAUDE. You're going to New York to see Susan in the play?

HANLON. We're flyin' in an hour.

MAIZEL. By plane.

VIRGIL. Take my advice, boys. Don't go. (*Sits on arm of chair.*)

MAUDE. (*Puzzled.*) Why shouldn't they?

HANLON. Yeah, why shouldn't we? Ain't the play any good.

VIRGIL. It's wonderful. I cried at every performance.

(*They* ALL *turn as* JOE *enters by front door.*)

MAUDE. The great playwright himself.

JOE. Nobody told me there was a party.

HANLON. Hiya, you big successful writer. How does it feel up there in them higher brackets?

JOE. The pain goes away finally. (*Indicating* HAN-LON's *clothes.*) Why the disguise?

HANLON. We don't want Broadway to think we're a couple of hicks from the sticks. I'm on the way to see our play.

JOE. You must tell me how it is. (*Notices* VIRGIL.) Well! Admiral Farragut is back.

VIRGIL. I thought you'd meet me at the airport in your new Mercedes-Benz.

JOE. I was there, but your plane didn't show up.

VIRGIL. We landed at Burbank.

JOE. My radar wasn't working.

(GEORGETTE *enters from kitchen with a bucket of ice.*)

What the hell is that on your head?

GEORGETTE. A hat.

JOE. So it is.

GEORGETTE. (*Crossing to bar.*) Will you be having dinner in?

JOE. Why?

GEORGETTE. We've run out of everything but whiskey. (*Puts down ice and starts back to kitchen.*)

JOE. (*To* VIRGIL.) What would you like for dinner?

VIRGIL. Anything's good enough for me—as long as it's New York cut steak, medium rare, with French fries and broccoli with melted butter.

MAUDE. No Jello?

JOE. (*To* GEORGETTE, *who stops at kitchen door.*) Make that for everybody. (*To* HANLON *and* MAIZEL.) Can you stay for dinner?

HANLON. And miss a free meal on the plane?

MAIZEL. I can stay long enough for another drink.

JOE. (*To* GEORGETTE.) Have you got money to go shopping?

GEORGETTE. We have a charge account.

HANLON. We'll be glad to give you a lift in the squad car.

GEORGETTE. No, thanks. If any of my friends ever saw me, I'd never live it down. (*Exits.*)

HANLON. (*To* JOE.) Got any message for the kid?

JOE. No message.

MAIZEL. That's easy to remember.

VIRGIL. I still say you shouldn't go.

HANLON. After I blow five hundred bucks on wardrobe and plane tickets? Not a chance! (*To* MAIZEL *at bar, who has bottle in his hand.*) Hey, man of distinction! Let's go!

(*He opens front door as* MAIZEL *comes around from bar with a bottle of champagne.* JOE *takes it from him as he passes, and* MAIZEL *exits.*)

(*Turning in doorway.*) I keep tellin' him not to drink on an empty head! Well—bon voyage! (*Exits.*)

JOE. (*To* VIRGIL.) Why didn't you want them to go see the show?

VIRGIL. (*Evasively.*) I'll tell you later.

JOE. Can't you tell me in front of Maude?

MAUDE. Is there something left that can't be said in front of me!

JOE. Well—what is it?

VIRGIL. (*Rising, starts for kitchen.*) We need some ice.

JOE. Georgette just put out ice.

VIRGIL. Wrong flavor. (*Exits into kitchen.*)

MAUDE. (*Rising.*) Okay—I'll leave. (*Crosses to get her coat.*) I know when I'm not wanted.

JOE. (*Helping her with coat.*) See you tomorrow. How's your mother?

MAUDE. I don't know yet. She won't be back from her honeymoon till Sunday. (*Crosses to front door.*)

JOE. What's this—her third?

MAUDE. Fourth. I think she's trying to set me a good example. (*Opens door, turns hesitantly.*) Joe?

JOE. Yes?

MAUDE. It's not too late.

JOE. Too late for what?

VIRGIL. (VIRGIL *enters from kitchen with two bottles of soda.*) Too late to save li'l ol' psychosomatic you.

JOE. Who's psychosomatic? I never looked better or felt better in my life.

MAUDE. Then you won't mind that I borrowed the last of your sleeping pills. The ones with the pretty little stripes.

JOE. They're extremely mild.

MAUDE. Like Chesterfields.

JOE. If you're in a hurry, Maude, you can take my car.

MAUDE. No, thanks. I think I'll walk. Maybe somebody'll pick me up. (*As the* MEN *look at each other.*) Well, I can dream, can't I? (*Exits.*)

JOE. (JOE *closes the door, then turns to* VIRGIL.) Okay—what's the big state secret?

VIRGIL. (*Crossing with soda to bar.*) Aren't you going to ask me about Susan?

JOE. (*Lighting cigarette.*) Susan? Oh, sure. How was she?

VIRGIL. Nervous as hell at rehearsals. Cool as a cucumber the minute the curtain went up.

JOE. What did she have to be nervous about! She was only playing herself.

VIRGIL. Did you hear about M-G-M? They want to test her.

JOE. (*Sits moodily on couch.*) They're crazy. She won't photograph.

VIRGIL. (*Crossing to him.*) No? You ought to be back there, Joe, taking bows with Susan. Why, she's the greatest thing since Wheaties! She could marry a million bucks tomorrow.

JOE. Could she? You know damn good and well the annulment didn't go through. Will you please tell me why she wouldn't sign the papers?

VIRGIL. Why don't you ask her? You'll like her, Joe— and you'll like the play. It's your best. I saw it six times—and I cried every time.

JOE. You cry at card tricks.

VIRGIL. Did you just make that up?

JOE. A writer never makes anything up. (*Rises irritably, paces while he talks.*) I'll tell you something else about my so-called profession. They say a writer's the luckiest person in the world. If anything bothers him, he puts it on paper and gets rid of it. I got a big piece of news for you—it ain't true.

VIRGIL. (*Pointedly.*) Can I translate that to mean that maybe you're in love with Susan?

JOE. (*Turning on him.*) I didn't say that.

VIRGIL. Well, batten down the hatches and call me a bo'sun's mate! When did you find out?

JOE. What's the difference?

VIRGIL. And the way I worked to make Susan hate you!

JOE. Thanks a lot.

VIRGIL. All those months she was taking dramatic lessons, I never missed a chance to take a rap at you— and your low character.

(*As* JOE *reacts.*)

When I saw her in New York, I even told her you were going out with Isabella again.

JOE. I don't care what you told her. You know I haven't seen Isabella since she got married. (*After pause.*) What was Susan's reaction?

VIRGIL. She made a date with a Peruvian millionaire.

JOE. (*Stretching out on couch.*) Look—I'm sick and tired of the whole thing. That's all anybody wants to talk about. Just forget about the play and Susan!

VIRGIL. Okay. They're forgotten. (*Starts for bedroom.*)

JOE. (*After a pause.*) Is she really going out with a Peruvian millionaire?

VIRGIL. (*Turning at bedroom door.*) Just for lunch at Sardi's, dinner at 21—and then after the show.

JOE. (*Righteously indignant, sits up.*) Doesn't he know she's a married woman?

VIRGIL. She doesn't seem to be working at it.

JOE. A married woman is a married woman.

VIRGIL. Well, that's a brilliant observation. Why didn't you tell Susan how you felt about her?

JOE. I—I didn't want a wife with a girlish crush on me. Or one who was grateful. (*Notices* VIRGIL's *bag.*) Why didn't you drop your bag off at your room?

VIRGIL. I've given up my room.

JOE. What for? You knew you'd be back in a week. And take your coat off—or are you having dinner in it?

VIRGIL. Sure. (*Starts to take off coat.*) Did I tell you I'm quitting?

JOE. What do you mean you're quitting?

VIRGIL. I'm firing myself.

JOE. What are you talking about?

VIRGIL. I've got a new job. (*Removes his coat. He is*

in the uniform of a Lieutenant in the Navy.) It's not really new.

JOE. (*Rises, speaks softly and sincerely.*) Nice to see you again, Mr. Roberts. What's the idea?

VIRGIL. I never had any feeling of security except in college or in the Navy. You've always kidded me about it, but I was a somebody in uniform. In civilian life I—well, I was just lucky you came along. To feed me and to spare me the facts of life.

JOE. Who figured that out for you?

VIRGIL. Susan, and she was right. (*Crossing to him.*) Let's face it, Joe. I don't belong in this town—and I'm not happy.

JOE. Move over.

VIRGIL. I've been trying for months to get back in, so I stopped off in Washington and made it official.

JOE. Deserter!

VIRGIL. You can send my food packages care of the Naval Base at San Diego.

JOE. (*Saluting.*) Aye, aye, sir. Any other orders?

VIRGIL. Yes. Why don't you get in the scramble for Susan? Maybe she'll see you in the crowd and come over.

JOE. (*Moving away.*) Not a chance.

VIRGIL. Why not?

JOE. (*Not turning to him.*) She'd come over to me, all right. I'm her husband. I'm the guy who took her off the streets. She'd feel she owed it to me. (*Turning to* VIRGIL.) I don't want it like that.

VIRGIL. (*Sighs.*) Well—I guess the Navy shouldn't meddle in civilian affairs.

(*There is a KNOCK on the front door.*)

JOE. Get that, will you?

(VIRGIL *gives him a Naval look.*)

I'm sorry, sir. I'll get it.

(JOE *goes to door, opens it.* SUSAN *stands in doorway. She wears a smart blue suit, gloves, a pert little hat with a half-veil. She is very much the well-dressed New Yorker. JOE looks at her for a long moment, then turns to VIRGIL.)*

There's a girl out here who looks a lot like Susan.

SUSAN. Maybe it is Susan.

JOE. *(Looks at watch.)* It can't be. She's due on stage in New York in about three hours.

SUSAN. She'll never make it. *(As JOE gapes at her.)* I was just passing through on my way to the prison farm. May I come in?

JOE. Looks like you are in.

(They watch her as she enters, takes off her hat, fluffs out her hair, sits nicely on the couch.)

SUSAN. It's easy to make an entrance after you've worked at it as long as I have.

JOE. Don't tell me the play closed.

SUSAN. Oh, no. They say it'll run at least two years.

JOE. Then why aren't you in New York?

SUSAN. *(Pulls gloves off slowly before she speaks.)* I couldn't wait two years.

JOE. *(The stupid male.)* Wait for what?

VIRGIL. Don't tell him, Susan. Let him guess.

SUSAN. Hi, Virgil. Are you back in the Navy?

JOE. No, he's in a revival of "The Student Prince."

SUSAN. Oh, that's too bad. *(Pointedly.)* I was going to ask him to run down and get my bags.

VIRGIL. *(Crossing to front door.)* I'll get them anyway. *(As he passes SUSAN.)* What kept you so long?

SUSAN. I wasted a whole day shopping for this hat.

VIRGIL. *(Admiringly.)* It was worth it. *(Exits, closes door.)*

JOE. *(Turns on SUSAN.)* Did Virgil know you were walking out on the play?

SUSAN. Of course. Didn't he tell you?

JOE. Nobody tells me anything around here! *(Fum-*

ing.) How can you walk out on a show—two weeks after it opens?

SUSAN. They replaced me.

JOE. What do you mean—they replaced you? That's crazy! You're the star!

SUSAN. My understudy went on last night. She was wonderful. She's a young kid from—Texas.

JOE. (JOE *faces her accusingly like a District Attorney.*) Equity will blackball you from coast to coast! Why did you do it?

SUSAN. I understand you've been going out with Isabella again.

JOE. You won't be able to get a split-week in a straw-hat theatre in the backwoods of Maine!

SUSAN. (*Unperturbed.*) Married men shouldn't go out with other women.

JOE. What about you and that Peruvian millionaire?

SUSAN. He's cute.

JOE. (*His temper gone by now.*) He's dangerous! All those Peruvian millionaires are.

SUSAN. That's the chance I have to take.

VIRGIL. (VIRGIL *enters by the front door with her bags.*) Where do these go?

SUSAN. In the bedroom.

VIRGIL. (*Crossing to bedroom.*) Would I like to be there when Sergeant Hanlon sees the understudy instead of Susan! (*Exits.*)

(SUSAN *starts to walk around the room, emptying one ash tray into another, rearranging things.*)

JOE. What do you think you're doing?

SUSAN. As long as I'm going to live here, I'd like a little tidier arrangement.

JOE. (*Following her.*) What makes you think you're going to live here?

SUSAN. I'm your wife.

JOE. Only technically. How many times did you go out with that Peruvian?

SUSAN. Do you still snore?

JOE. Miss Landis, I asked you how many—

SUSAN. (*Interrupting.*) Mrs. Norton.

JOE. I'm not going to go through that again.

SUSAN. (*Stops, turns to face him.*) Why don't you admit you can't live without me—and that you're glad I'm back?

JOE. Because I'm stupid.

SUSAN. I won't argue the point. Why don't you, really?

JOE. (*Stuck.*) Because—because I'm thirty-four going on thirty-five. (*Crosses to couch and sits.*)

SUSAN. You're twenty-nine going on thirty.

JOE. I've aged five years since you walked in here.

SUSAN. (SUSAN *crosses to couch, sits beside* JOE.) Do you know why I came back?

JOE. Because you're grateful.

SUSAN. No, because a marriage never works when two people are three thousand miles apart.

JOE. (*Rises when she moves closer.*) I don't remember writing that in the play.

SUSAN. You don't remember a lot of things. Like the first time you kissed me. Under the mistletoe.

JOE. I remember.

SUSAN. (*Rises, goes over to him.*) Do you?

JOE. And I also remember you're only—you didn't lie to me about your age, did you?

SUSAN. I was eighteen in August.

JOE. And I'll be thirty-five in November! (*Turns on her and* SUSAN *backs away as he goes into a tirade.*) Does an eighteen-year-old girl realize what she's doing when she marries a man nearly thirty-five? You haven't given a thought to the fact that when I'm fifty you'll be only—thirty-three. A woman in her prime—in full flower! You'll be at the age when you'll want and need your husband most. And where will *I* be? *Over the hill!!*

SUSAN. We all have to go sometime.

JOE. And when I'm sixty, how old will you be?

SUSAN. Forty-three!

JOE. *The dangerous age!* Will you be satisfied to stay home and take care of all the imaginary illnesses of a man of sixty? No—you'll want to go out and live. And *me?* I'll be just around the corner from Social Security!

SUSAN. I've never heard such a brilliant presentation of the basic facts.

(VIRGIL *enters from the bedroom, salutes to* SUSAN, *who salutes back.* VIRGIL *crosses to front door, picking up valet pack enroute.*)

JOE. And another thing you may not be aware of, my dear young lady!

(SUSAN *has backed toward the bedroom.* JOE *follows her, unaware to where she is leading him.*)

Love isn't based on a silly girlish infatuation. Maybe in the movies but not in real life. There's a whole lot more to it than that! There has to be a mutual need and a mutual want and a mutual desire!

SUSAN. Who's arguing?

(*She backs into the bedroom.* JOE *reacts, exits after her, closes door.* VIRGIL *takes the phone off the hook, puts it on the desk, exits by front door.*)

CURTAIN

SUSAN SLEPT HERE

PROPERTY PLOT

FURNITURE

ACT ONE, SCENE 1

Desk, stage Right
Waste paper basket under desk
Modern chair behind desk
Modern chair Left of desk
Modern couch down Left Center
Small modern pillows on couch
Coffee table front of couch
Chair, stage Left
End table
Lamp on end table
Bar, stage Left
Bar stool, stage Left
Table by window
Lamp on table by window
Bookcases up stage Right and Left
Ottomans next to coffee table
Small table, stage Right
Modern chair, stage Right
Decorated and lighted Christmas tree up stage Right
Coat and umbrella rack
Vases for flowers
  On desk:
Ashtray
Cigarettes
Cigarette lighter
Lamp

Portable typewriter
Yellow paper, carbon paper
Pencils, miscellaneous desk paraphernalia
Telephone with long extension cord
Framed picture of beautiful girl
  On coffee table:
Cigarettes
Cigarette lighter
Ashtray
Magazines
Books
Wrapped Christmas packages
Christmas ribbons and seals
Scissors
Scotch tape
  On bar:
Decanter of Scotch
Decanter of Bourbon
6 highball glasses
6 old-fashioned glasses
6 cocktail glasses
Ice bucket
Cigarettes
Cigarette lighter
Bottle opener
4 bottles of soda
4 bottles of coca-cola
  Off Left:
Joe's flannel robe
Joe's bedroom slippers
Joe's fresh suit, shirt, tie, shoes
Joe's topcoat
  Over bar:
Mistletoe
  Off Right:
Georgette's raincoat and galoshes
Tray with liverwurst sandwich, glass of milk, small bowl
    fruit

Off Center:
Water to wet down slickers
 Effects off:
Buzzer for phone
Automobile horn
 On coat and umbrella rack:
Maude's raincoat and umbrella
 In desk drawer:
2 decks of cards
Gin rummy score pad and pencil

ACT ONE, SCENE 2

 On couch:
Blanket
Pillow
 Off Center:
Suit-box
 Off Right:
Table cloth and tray
Knife, fork, spoon
Napkin
Breakfast plate
Coffee cups and saucers
Egg cup
Boiled egg
Salt and pepper shakers
Slices buttered toast
Cream pitcher
Sugar bowl
 Off Left:
Large bath towel
Joe's jacket, slacks, sport shirt
Joe's topcoat
Susan's skirt, blouse, high-heeled shoes, Mexican rebosa
Susan's complete first wardrobe
 Effects off:
Dish-crash effect

ACT TWO, SCENE 1

On couch:
Newspapers
2 suitcases
Joe's clothes in suitcases
In vases:
Fresh flowers
On desk:
Portable typewriter in carrying case
Off Left:
Susan's first wardrobe except slicker and hat
Joe's shirts and ties
Off Center:
2 matching bridal bouquets
Pair of skis
Off Right:
2 cups of coffee
Ham sandwich
Cheese sandwich
Breakfast tray
Fried eggs, toast, coffee
Susan's slicker and hat

ACT TWO, SCENE 2

Off:
Christmas tree
Mistletoe
Flowers
Coffee cups
Newspapers
On coffee table:
Text books
School notebook
Typed term paper
Off Right:
Salami sandwich on plate
Napkin
Cup of coffee

Off Left:
Susan's dress
Cigarette in holder
Papers for briefcase
   Off Center Right:
Briefcase
   In desk drawer:
Letter and envelope

ACT TWO, SCENE 3

   Off:
Text books
School notebook
Typed term paper
Ice bucket
Soda on bar
On desk:
Scrap book
New York newspaper clippings
The *New Yorker*
   On bar:
Hat-box
Hat
Bottle of champagne
   Off Center:
Virgil's valet pack (red plaid)
Large suitcase ⎱
Make up bag ⎰ matched set
   Off Right:
Ice bucket
2 bottles of soda

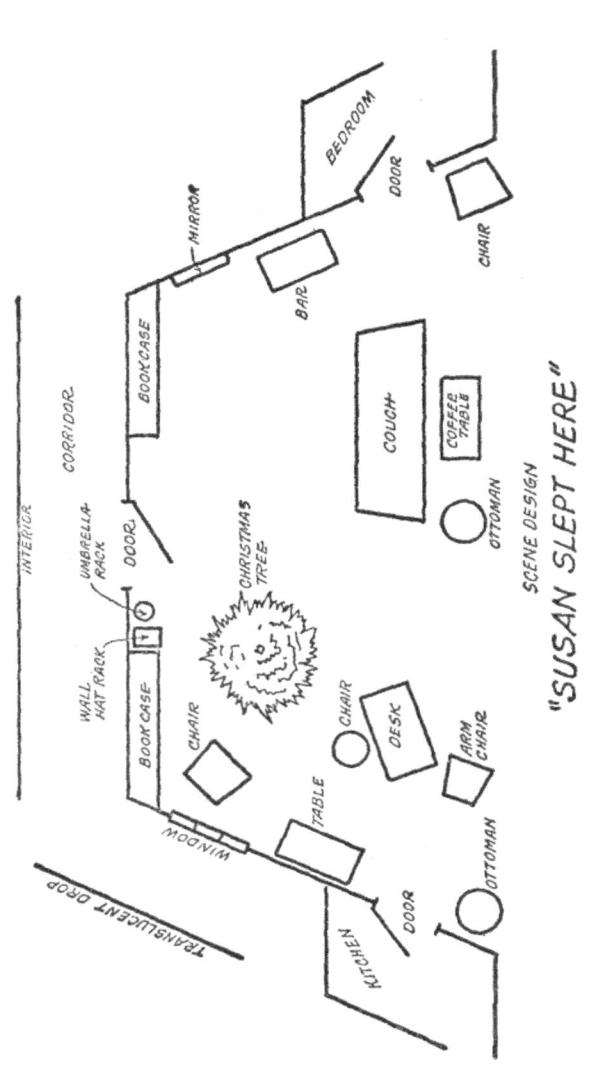

SCENE DESIGN

"SUSAN SLEPT HERE"

INTERIOR

CORRIDOR

TRANSLUCENT DROP

BOOKCASE

MIRROR

BAR

BEDROOM

DOOR

CHAIR

COUCH

COFFEE TABLE

OTTOMAN

DOOR

UMBRELLA RACK

WALL HAT RACK

BOOK CASE

CHRISTMAS TREE

CHAIR

CHAIR

DESK

ARM CHAIR

WINDOW

TABLE

OTTOMAN

KITCHEN

DOOR

SUSAN SLEPT HERE

STORY OF THE PLAY

On a rainy Christmas Eve successful 35-year-old Hollywood writer Joe Norton gets an unexpected present from a detective friend for use as research material—a 17-year-old juvenile delinquent named Susan! His pal Virgil, Joe's commanding officer in the Navy who now works for Joe, leaves and Joe is stuck with Susan.

The next morning he learns Susan's life story, decides he won't let her be sent to the prison farm, talks Susan into flying to Las Vegas and marrying him. Before she wakes up after their all-night ride back, Joe leaves for his mountain cabin to write a play about Susan. Virgil, aided by a call from Joe, talks Susan into staying and taking dramatic lessons.

The play doesn't jell until Joe returns and Susan gives him the right slant with a letter from her mother. Just when she thinks she's won her man again, back he goes to the mountains.

The play opens and Susan becomes the talk of Broadway. Joe won't admit he loves and misses her. Virgil returns from seeing the play, reveals he's re-enlisted to show he can stand on his own two feet.

Susan appears, mature, poised. She's walked out of the play to be with Joe, and she doesn't have too much trouble convincing him that age differentials mean nothing when two people love each other. As Susan backs Joe into the bedroom, Virgil thoughtfully takes the phone off the hook and exits.